# Kat & Mouse

## 1 teacher torture

Story by Alex de Campi
Art by Federica Manfredi

TOKYOPOP®
HAMBURG // LONDON // LOS ANGELES // TOKYO
Spotlight

**visit us at www.abdopublishing.com**

Reinforced library bound edition published in 2009 by Spotlight, a division of ABDO Publishing Group, 8000 West 78th Street, Edina, Minnesota 55439. This edition reprinted by arrangement with TOKYOPOP Inc. www.tokyopop.com



| | |
|---|---|
| Written by | Alex de Campi |
| Illustrated by | Federica Manfredi |
| Tones | Kathy Schilling |
| Lettering | Erika "Skooter" Terriquez |
| Cover Design | Anne Marie Horne |
| Editor | Carol Fox |
| Digital Imaging Manager | Chris Buford |

**Library of Congress Cataloging-in-Publication Data**

De Campi, Alex.

Kat & Mouse / story by Alex de Campi ; art by Federica Manfredi. -- Reinforced library bound ed.

v. cm.

Summary: Collects three previously published manga volumes in which classmates Kat Foster and Mee-Seen "Mouse" Huang investigate events involving their private school, Dover Academy, and a mysterious thief known as the Artful Dodger.

Contents: Teacher torture -- Tripped -- The ice storm.

ISBN 978-1-59961-564-6 (vol. 1: Teacher torture : alk. paper)

1. Graphic novels. [1. Graphic novels. 2. Schools--Fiction. 3. Friendship--Fiction. 4. Robbers and outlaws--Fiction. 5. Mystery and detective stories.] I. Manfredi, Federica, ill. II. Title. III. Title: Kat and Mouse.

PZ7.7.D32Kat 2009

[Fic]--dc22 2008002189

Spotlight

All Spotlight books have reinforced library binding and are manufactured in the United States of America.

Kat & Mouse

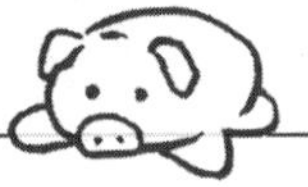

# TABLE OF CONTENTS



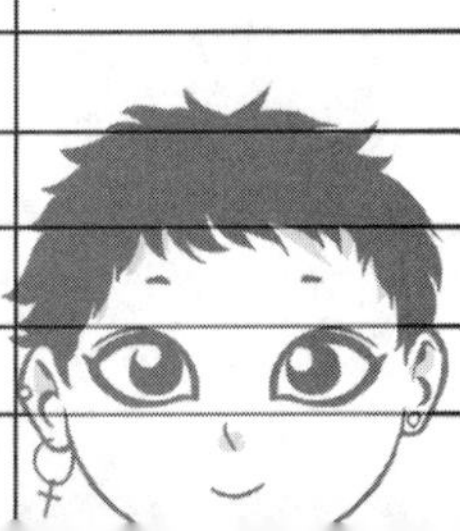

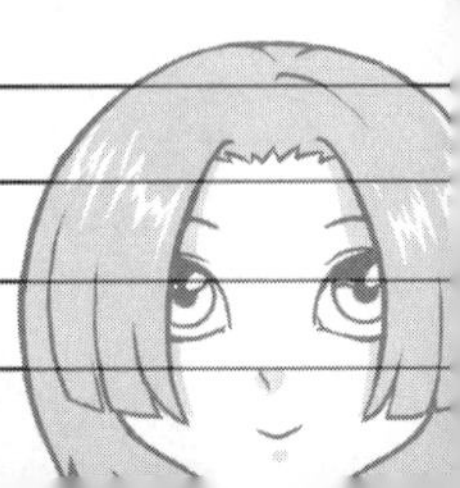

# Chapter 1: The Best and Brightest

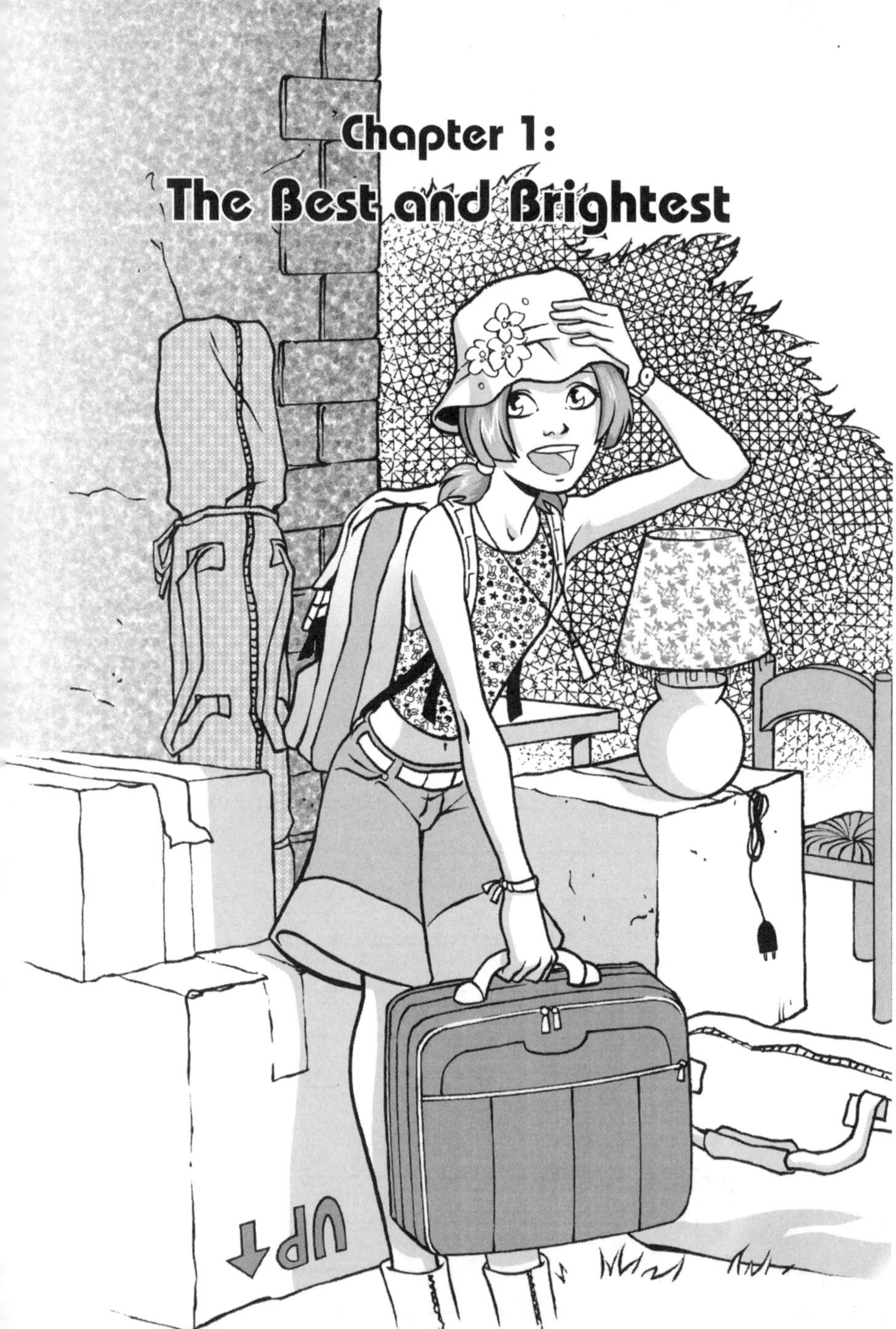
UP

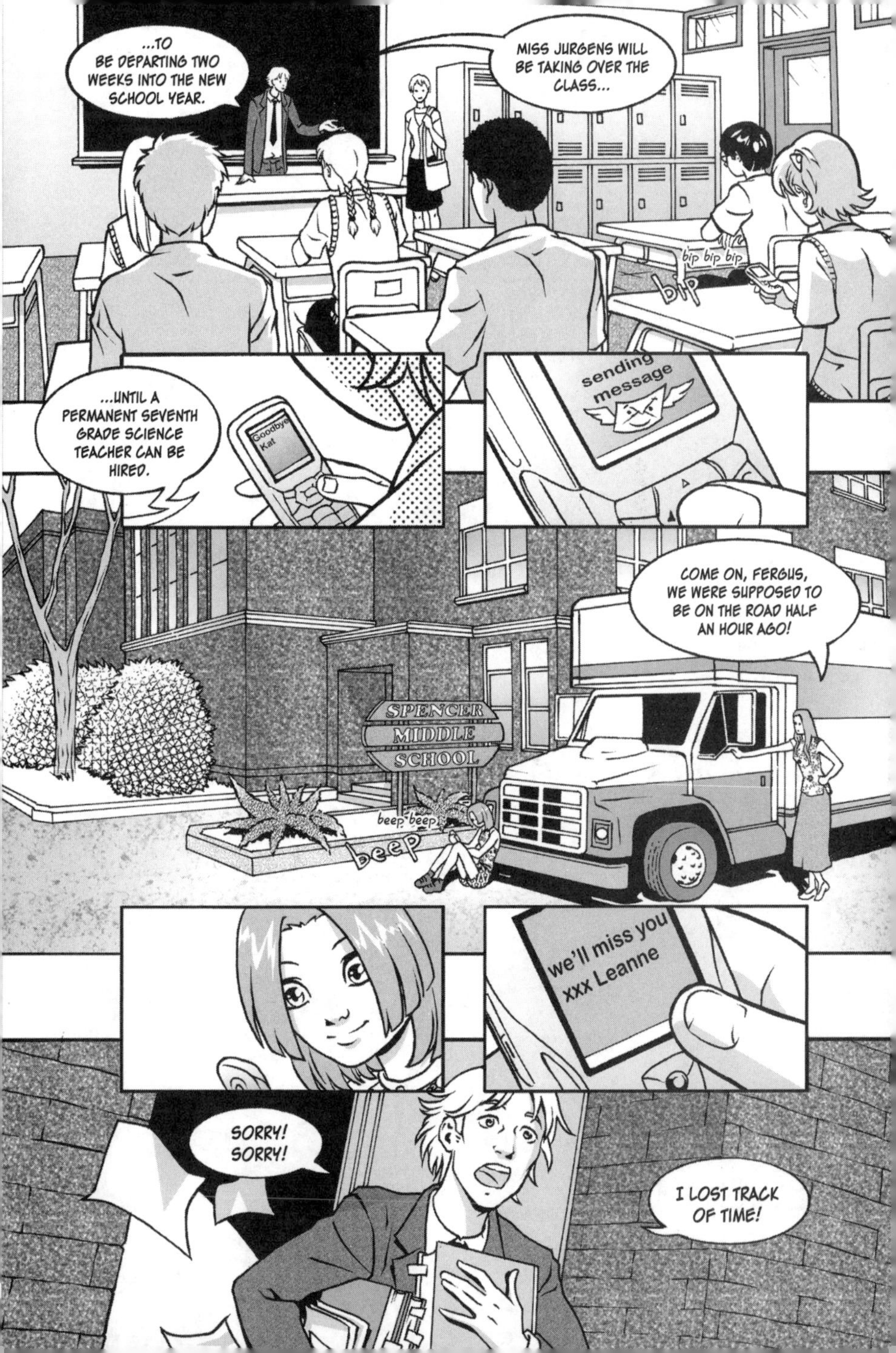
...TO BE DEPARTING TWO WEEKS INTO THE NEW SCHOOL YEAR.
MISS JURGENS WILL BE TAKING OVER THE CLASS...
bip bip bip
bip
...UNTIL A PERMANENT SEVENTH GRADE SCIENCE TEACHER CAN BE HIRED.
Goodbye Kat
sending message
COME ON, FERGUS, WE WERE SUPPOSED TO BE ON THE ROAD HALF AN HOUR AGO!
SPENCER MIDDLE SCHOOL
beep beep
beep
we'll miss you xxx Leanne
SORRY! SORRY!
I LOST TRACK OF TIME!

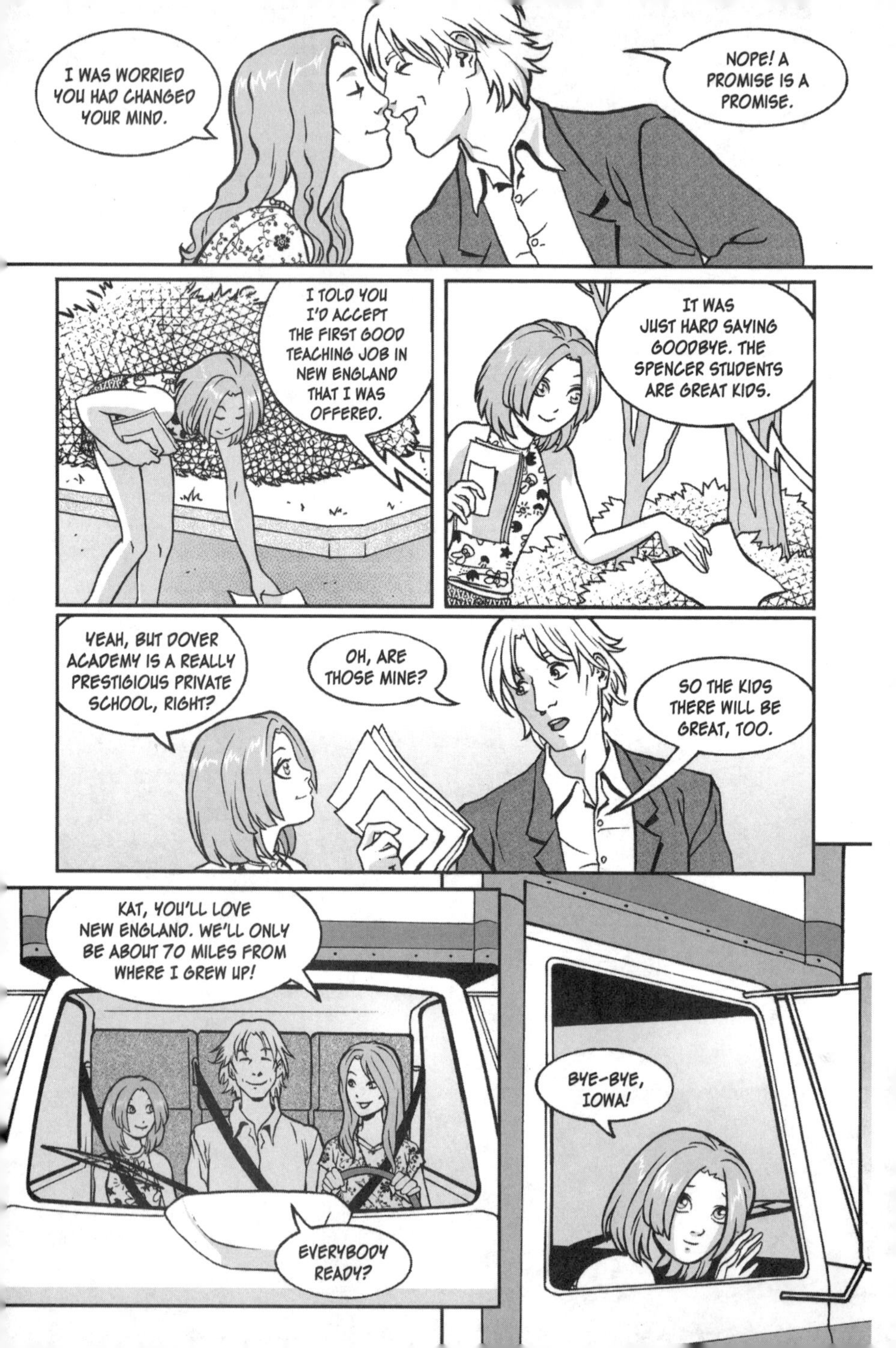
I WAS WORRIED YOU HAD CHANGED YOUR MIND.
NOPE! A PROMISE IS A PROMISE.
I TOLD YOU I'D ACCEPT THE FIRST GOOD TEACHING JOB IN NEW ENGLAND THAT I WAS OFFERED.
IT WAS JUST HARD SAYING GOODBYE. THE SPENCER STUDENTS ARE GREAT KIDS.
YEAH, BUT DOVER ACADEMY IS A REALLY PRESTIGIOUS PRIVATE SCHOOL, RIGHT?
OH, ARE THOSE MINE?
SO THE KIDS THERE WILL BE GREAT, TOO.
KAT, YOU'LL LOVE NEW ENGLAND. WE'LL ONLY BE ABOUT 70 MILES FROM WHERE I GREW UP!
EVERYBODY READY?
BYE-BYE, IOWA!

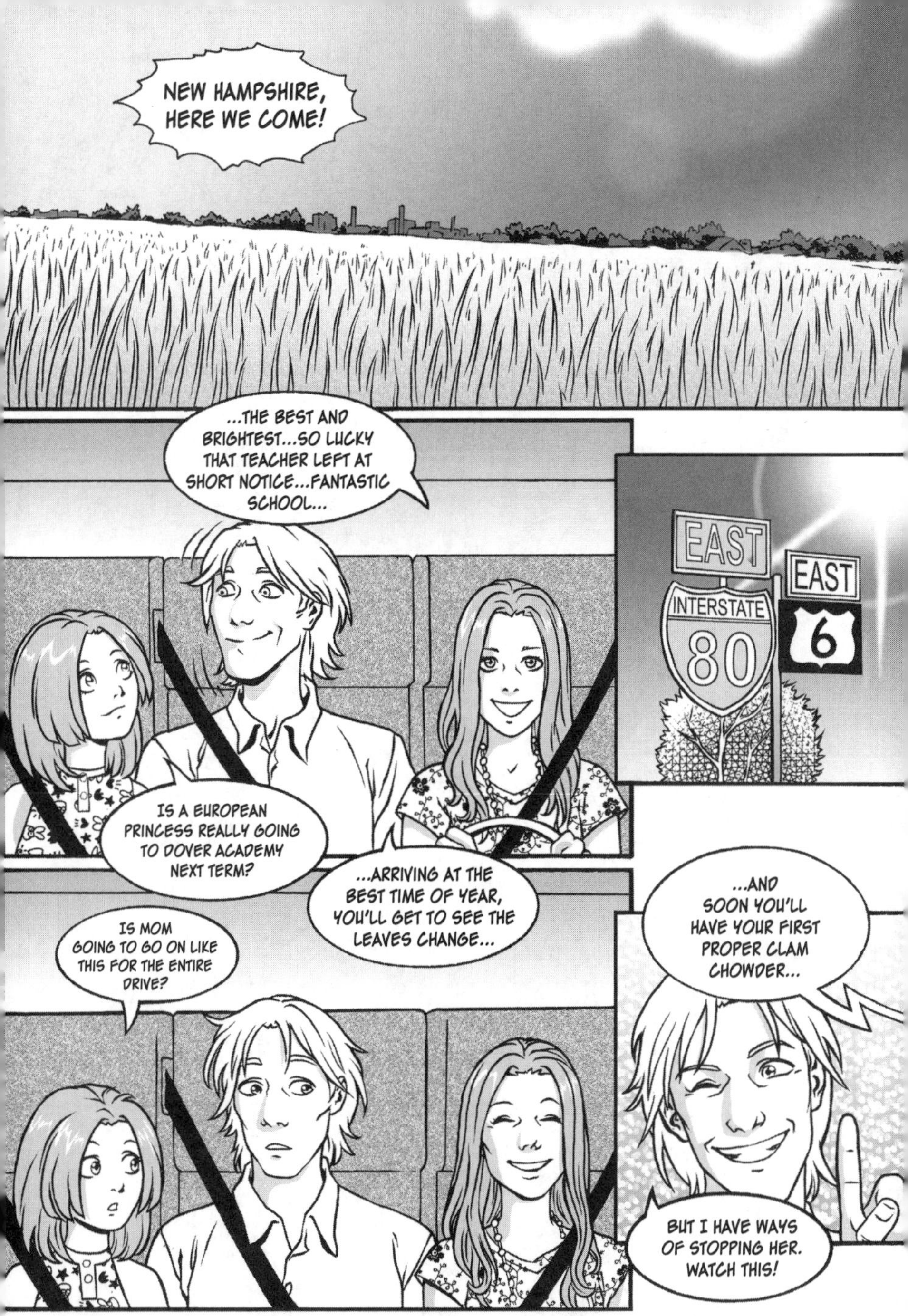

NEW HAMPSHIRE, HERE WE COME!
...THE BEST AND BRIGHTEST...SO LUCKY THAT TEACHER LEFT AT SHORT NOTICE...FANTASTIC SCHOOL...
IS A EUROPEAN PRINCESS REALLY GOING TO DOVER ACADEMY NEXT TERM?
EAST
INTERSTATE
80
EAST
6
...ARRIVING AT THE BEST TIME OF YEAR, YOU'LL GET TO SEE THE LEAVES CHANGE...
IS MOM GOING TO GO ON LIKE THIS FOR THE ENTIRE DRIVE?
...AND SOON YOU'LL HAVE YOUR FIRST PROPER CLAM CHOWDER...
BUT I HAVE WAYS OF STOPPING HER. WATCH THIS!

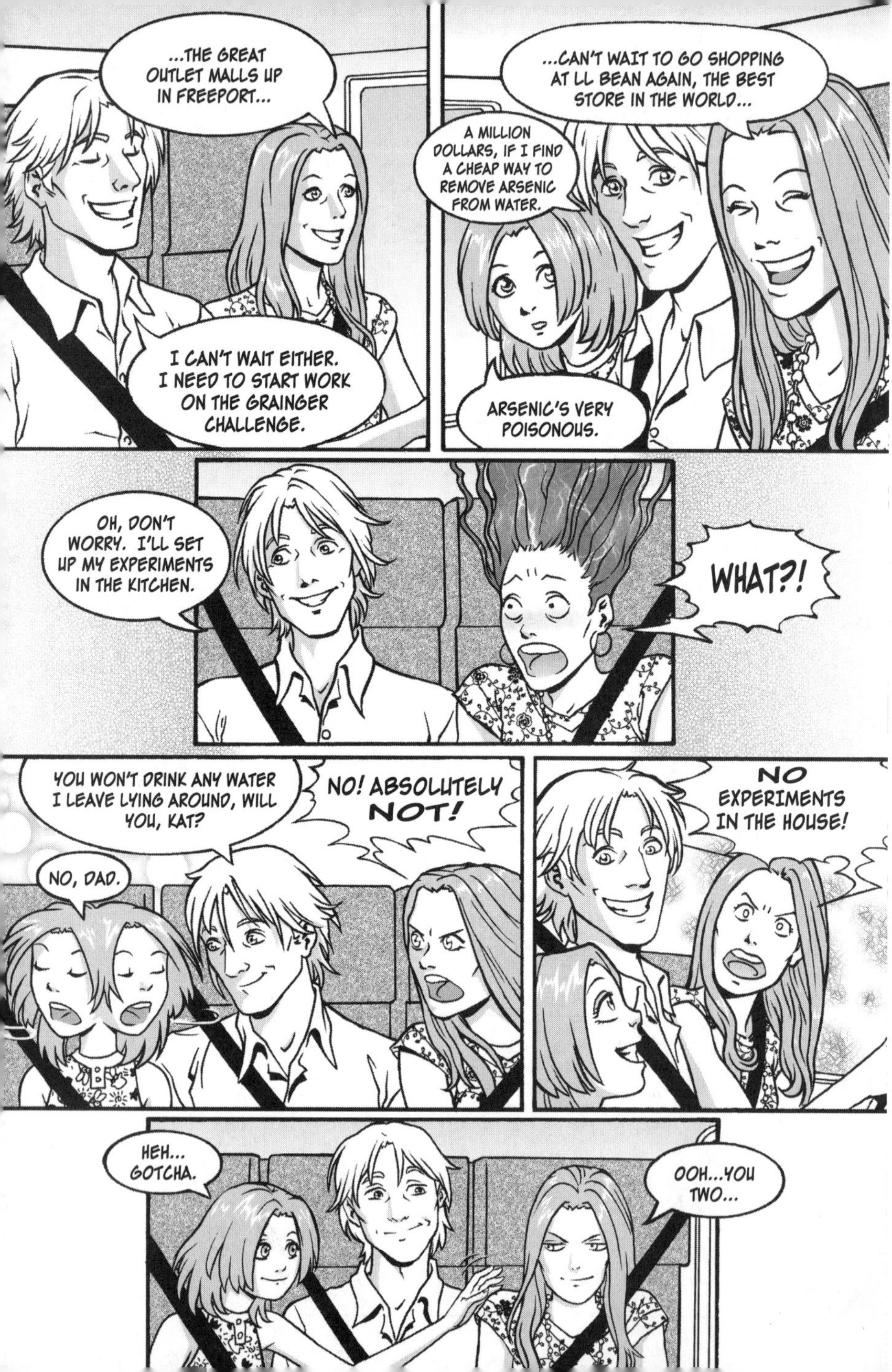
...THE GREAT OUTLET MALLS UP IN FREEPORT...
I CAN'T WAIT EITHER. I NEED TO START WORK ON THE GRAINGER CHALLENGE.
...CAN'T WAIT TO GO SHOPPING AT LL BEAN AGAIN, THE BEST STORE IN THE WORLD...
A MILLION DOLLARS, IF I FIND A CHEAP WAY TO REMOVE ARSENIC FROM WATER.
ARSENIC'S VERY POISONOUS.
OH, DON'T WORRY. I'LL SET UP MY EXPERIMENTS IN THE KITCHEN.
WHAT?!
YOU WON'T DRINK ANY WATER I LEAVE LYING AROUND, WILL YOU, KAT?
NO, DAD.
NO! ABSOLUTELY NOT!
NO EXPERIMENTS IN THE HOUSE!
HEH... GOTCHA.
OOH...YOU TWO...

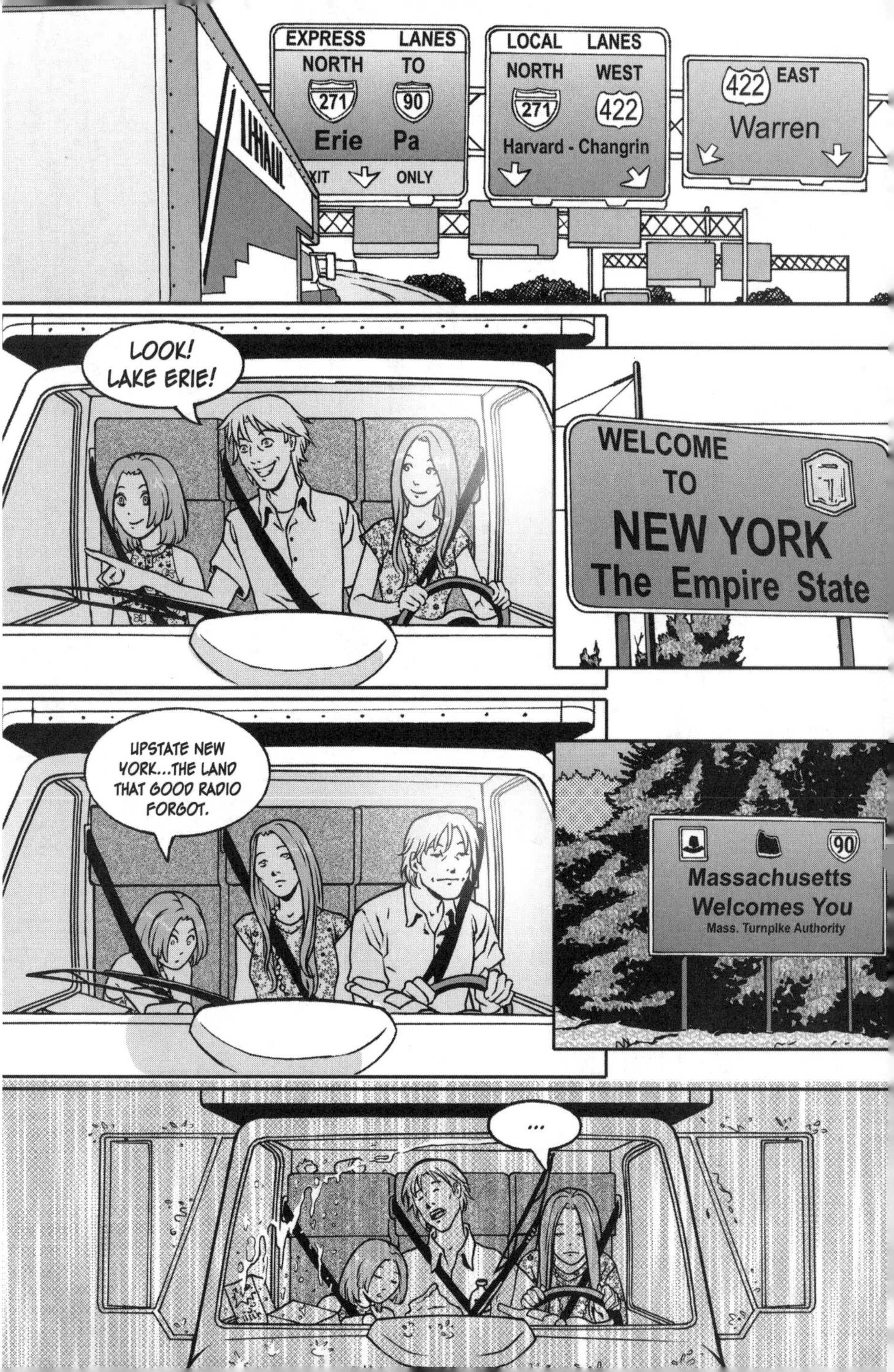
EXPRESS LANES
NORTH 271 TO 90
Erie Pa
XIT ONLY
LOCAL LANES
NORTH 271 WEST 422
Harvard - Changrin
422 EAST
Warren
LOOK! LAKE ERIE!
WELCOME TO NEW YORK The Empire State
UPSTATE NEW YORK...THE LAND THAT GOOD RADIO FORGOT.
90
Massachusetts Welcomes You
Mass. Turnpike Authority
...

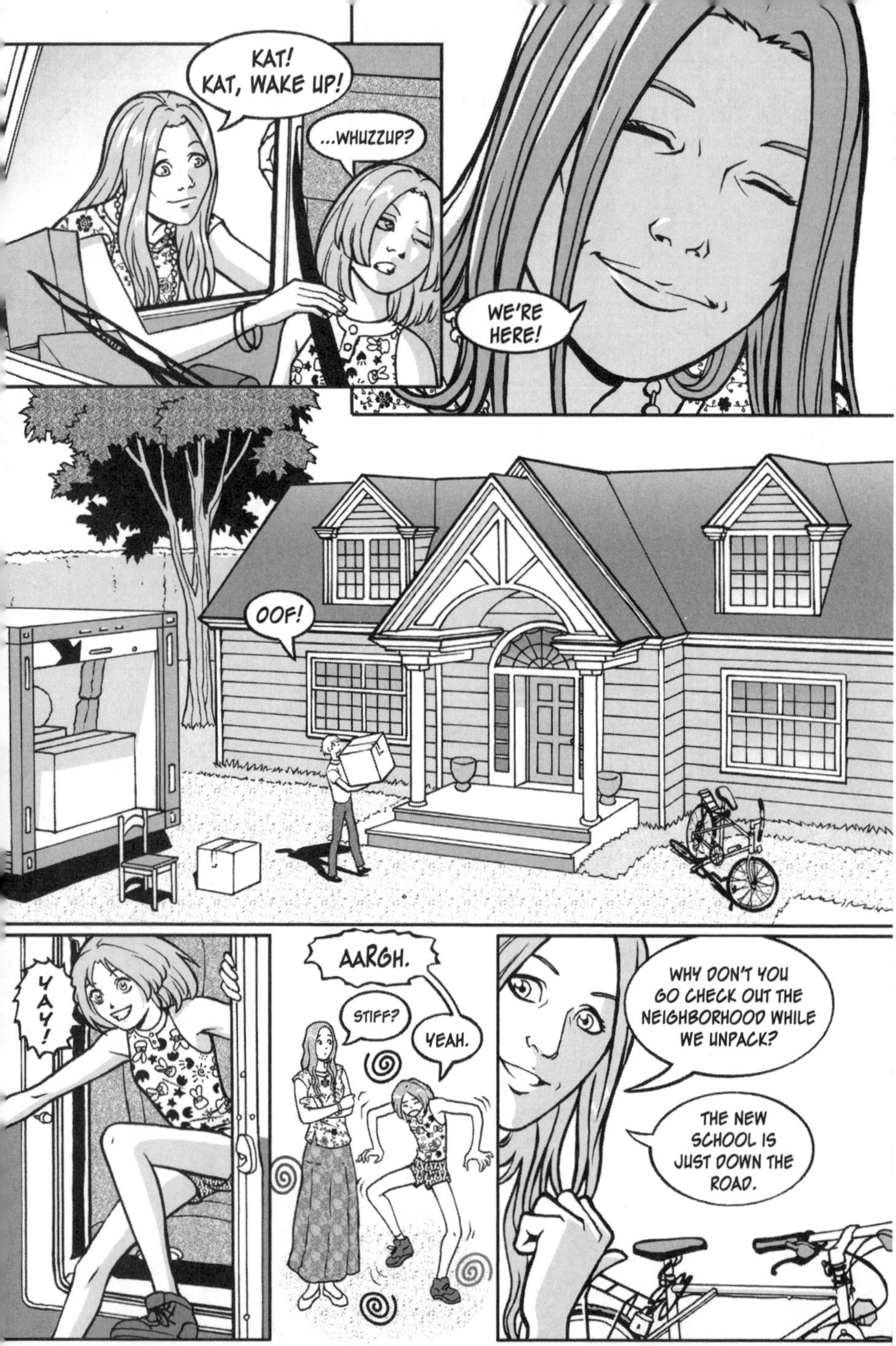
KAT! KAT, WAKE UP!
...WHUZZUP?
WE'RE HERE!
OOF!
YAY!
AARGH.
STIFF?
YEAH.
WHY DON'T YOU GO CHECK OUT THE NEIGHBORHOOD WHILE WE UNPACK?
THE NEW SCHOOL IS JUST DOWN THE ROAD.

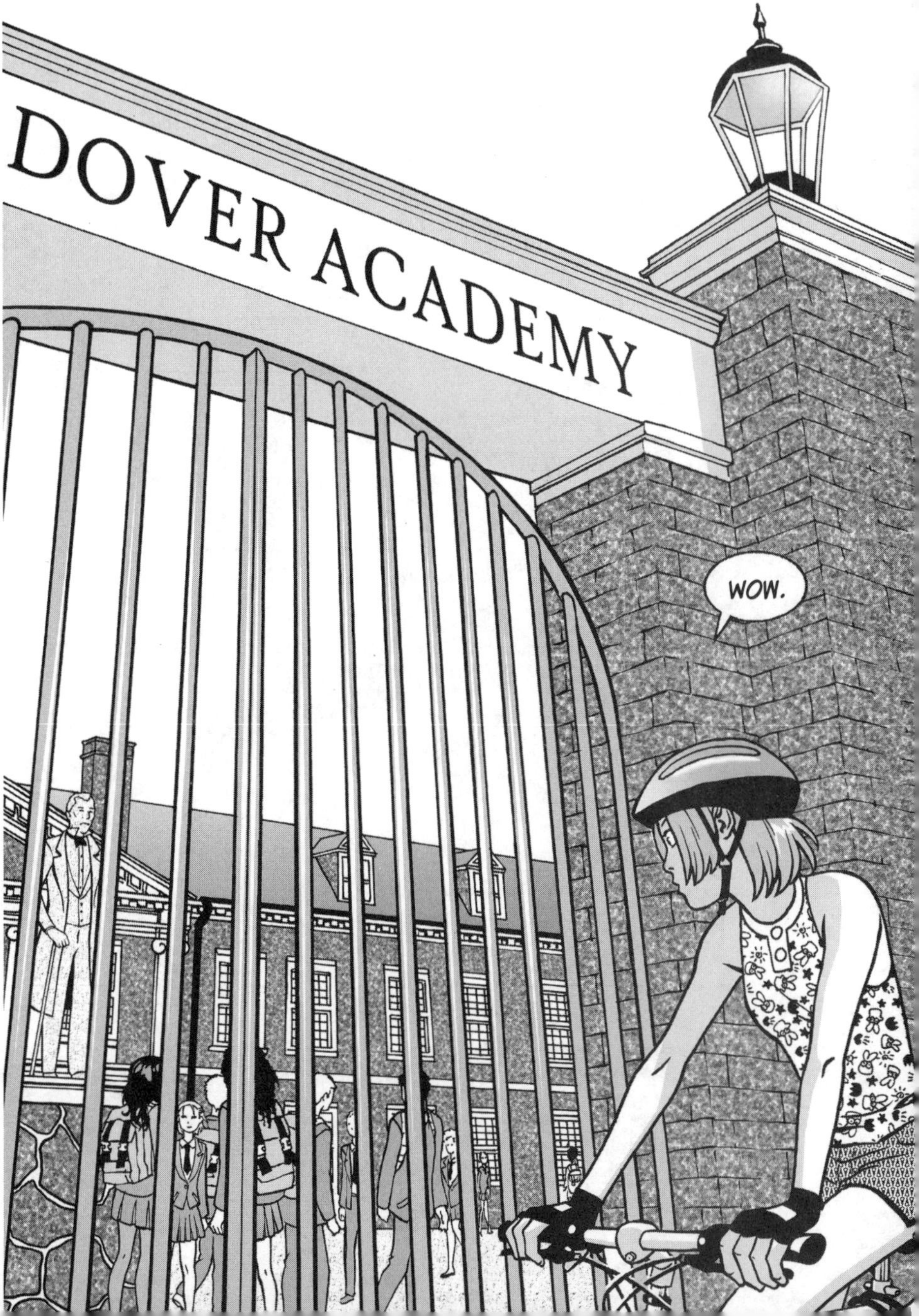
DOVER ACADEMY
WOW.

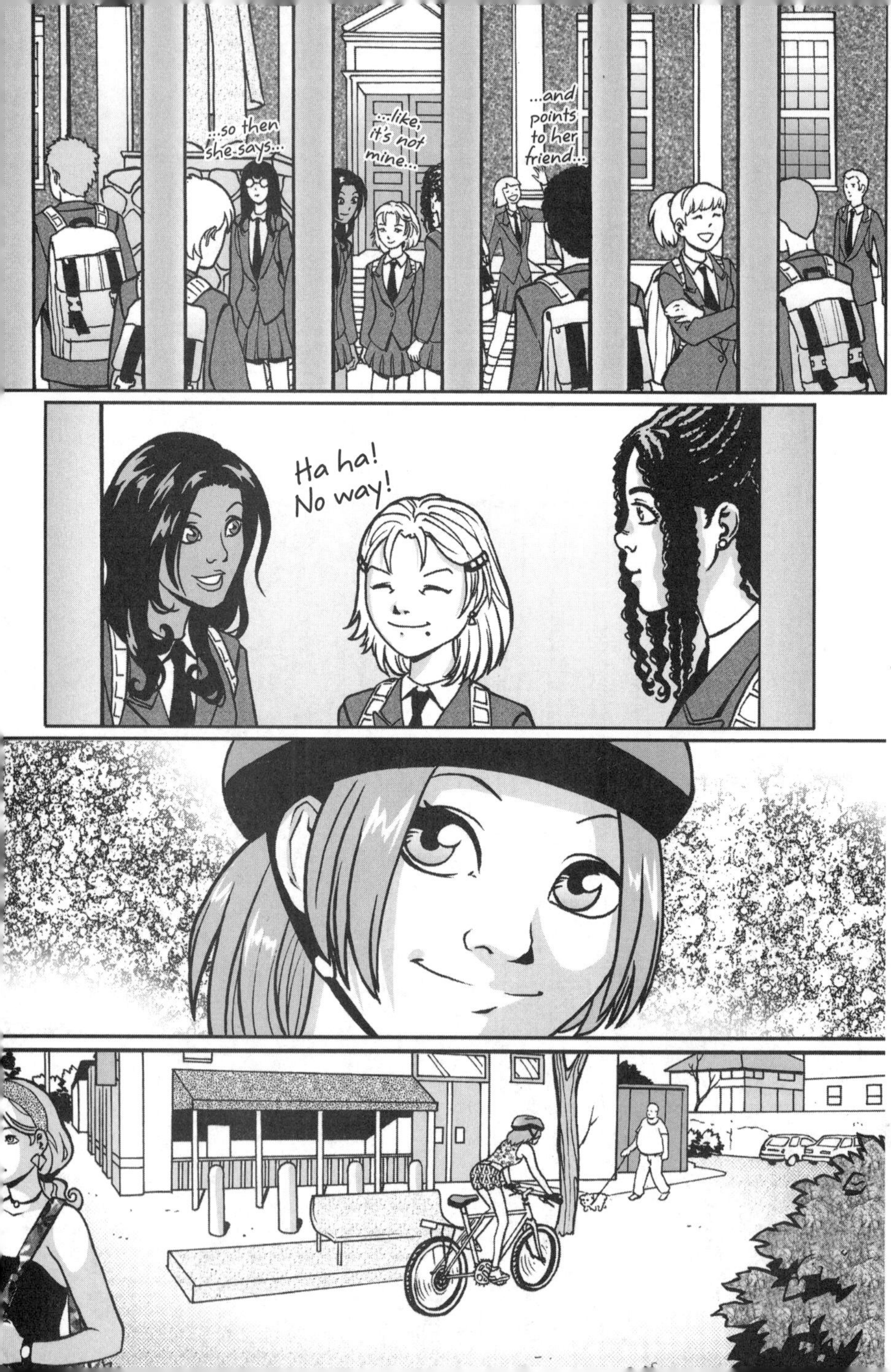
...so then she says...
...like, it's not mine...
...and points to her friend...
Ha ha! No way!

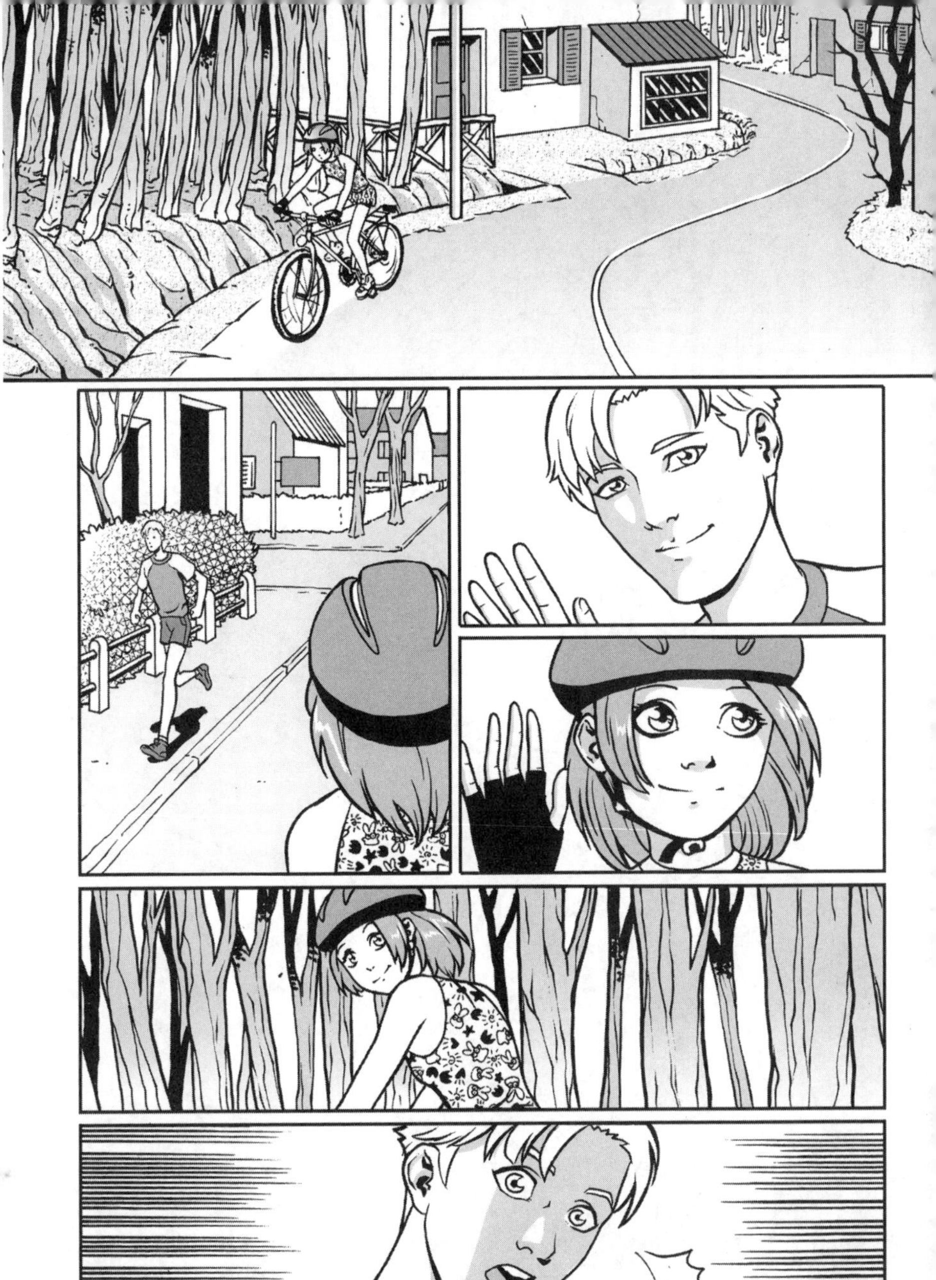

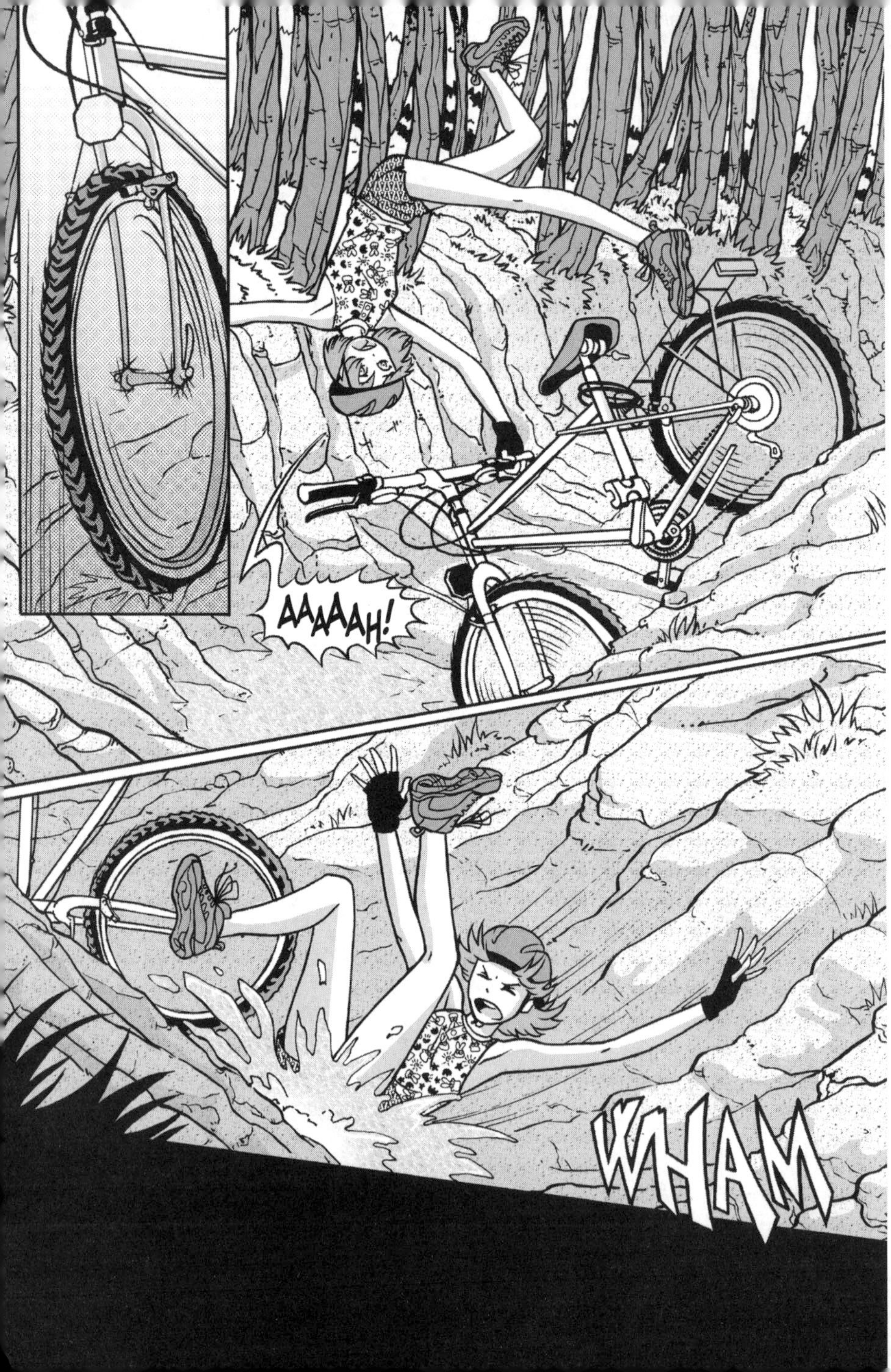

AAAAAH!
WHAM

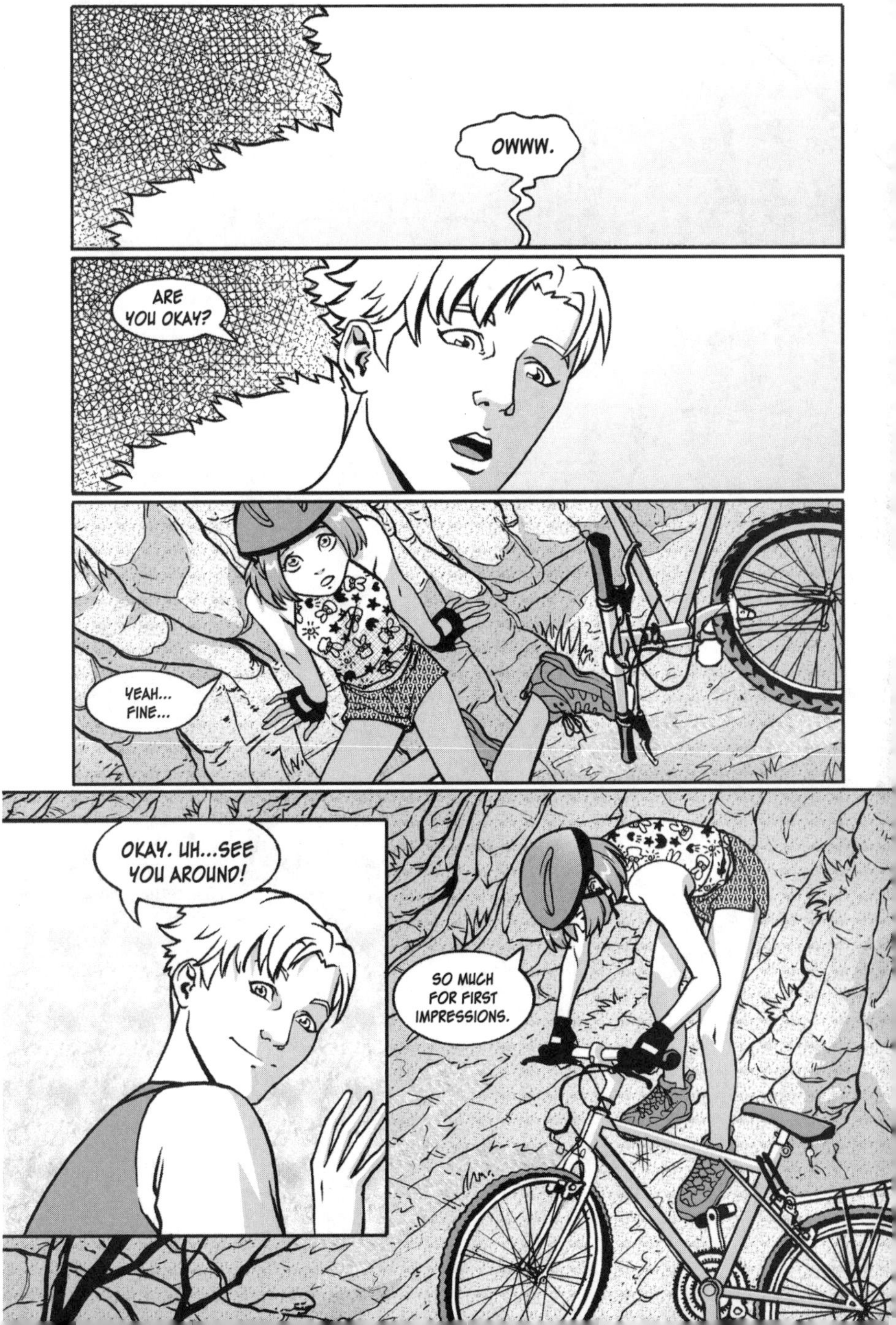
OWWW.
ARE YOU OKAY?
YEAH... FINE...
OKAY. UH...SEE YOU AROUND!
SO MUCH FOR FIRST IMPRESSIONS.

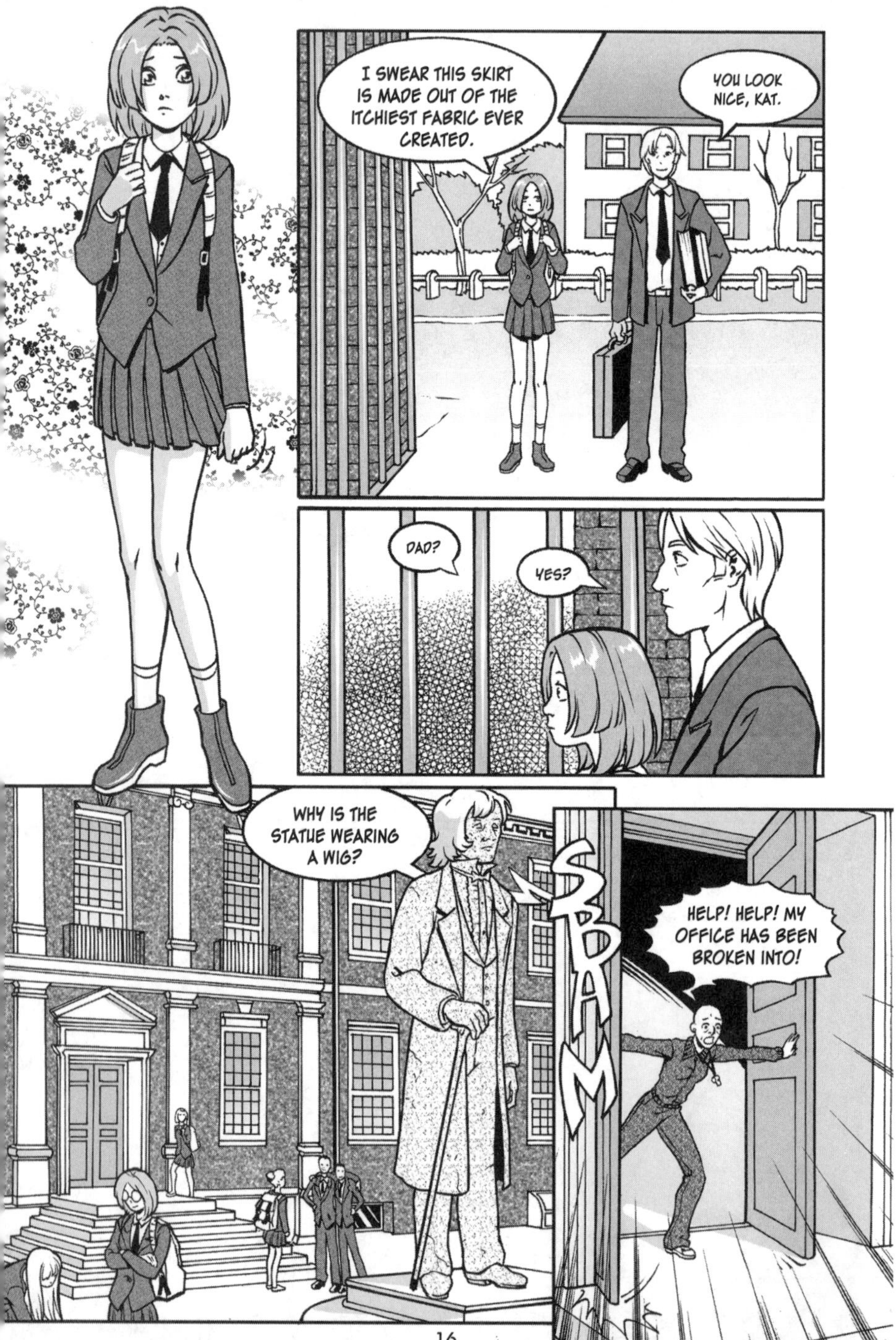

I SWEAR THIS SKIRT IS MADE OUT OF THE ITCHIEST FABRIC EVER CREATED.
YOU LOOK NICE, KAT.
DAD?
YES?
WHY IS THE STATUE WEARING A WIG?
SBAM
HELP! HELP! MY OFFICE HAS BEEN BROKEN INTO!

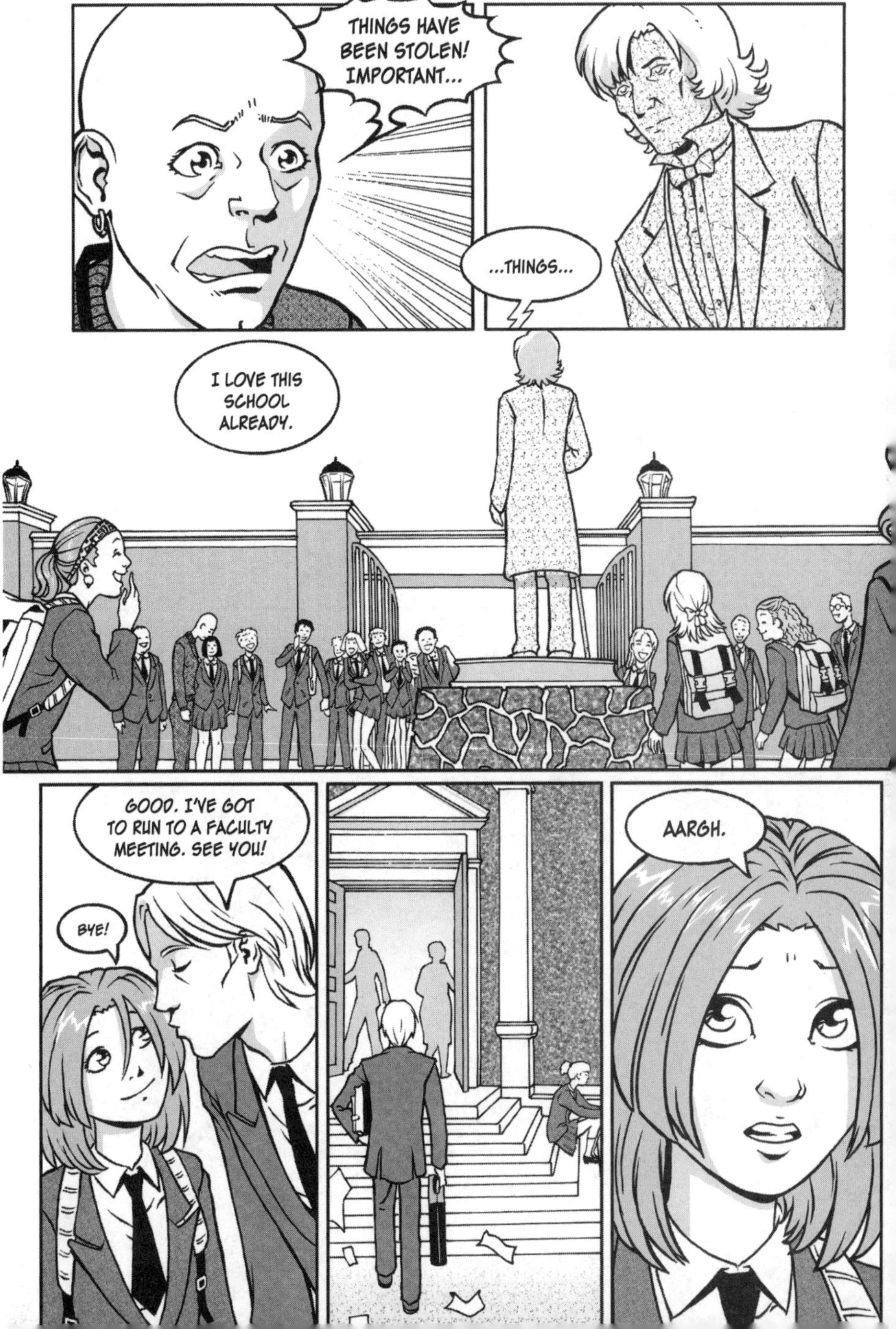
THINGS HAVE BEEN STOLEN! IMPORTANT...
...THINGS...
I LOVE THIS SCHOOL ALREADY.
GOOD. I'VE GOT TO RUN TO A FACULTY MEETING. SEE YOU!
BYE!
AARGH.

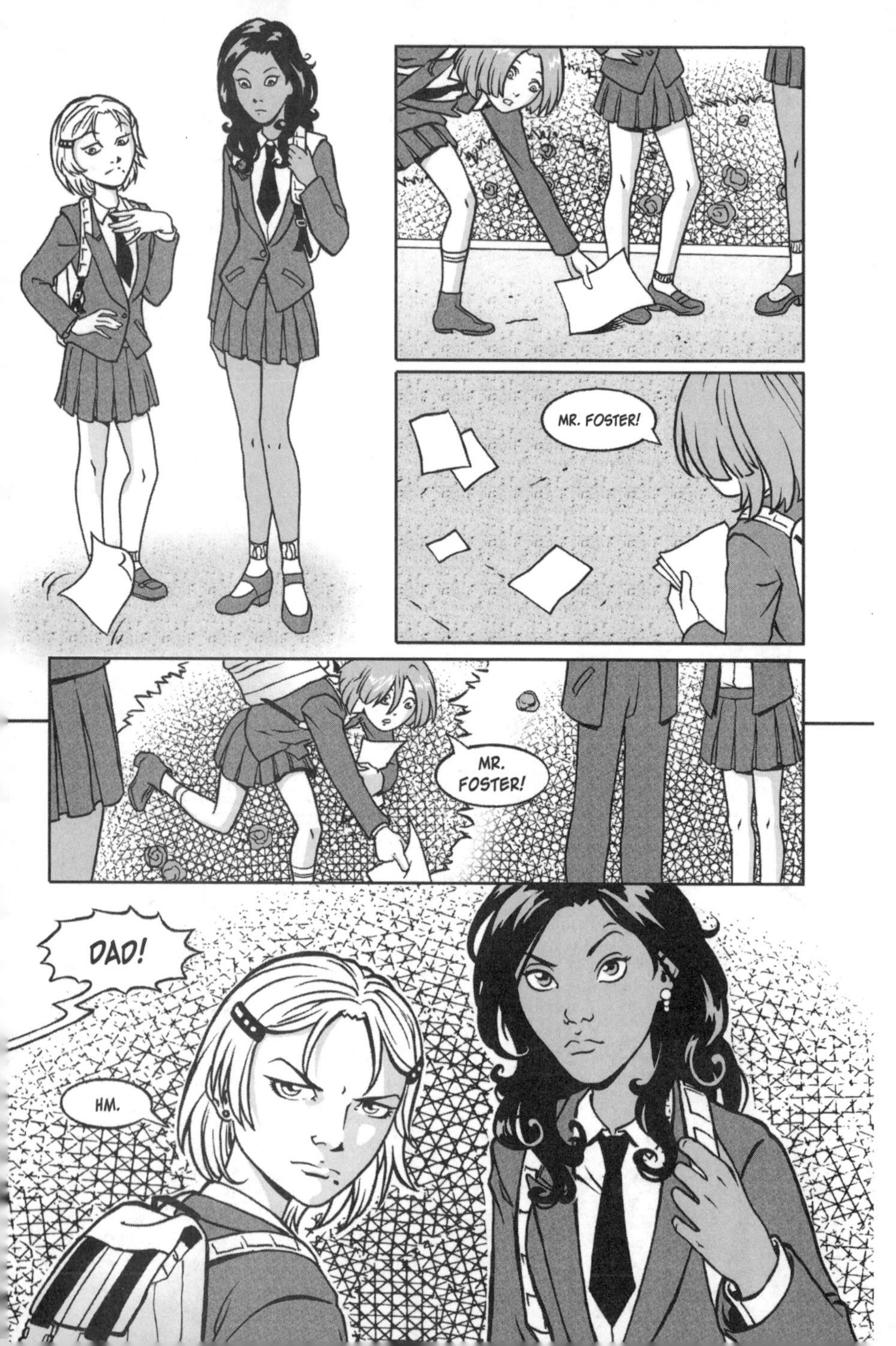
MR. FOSTER!
MR. FOSTER!
DAD!
HM.

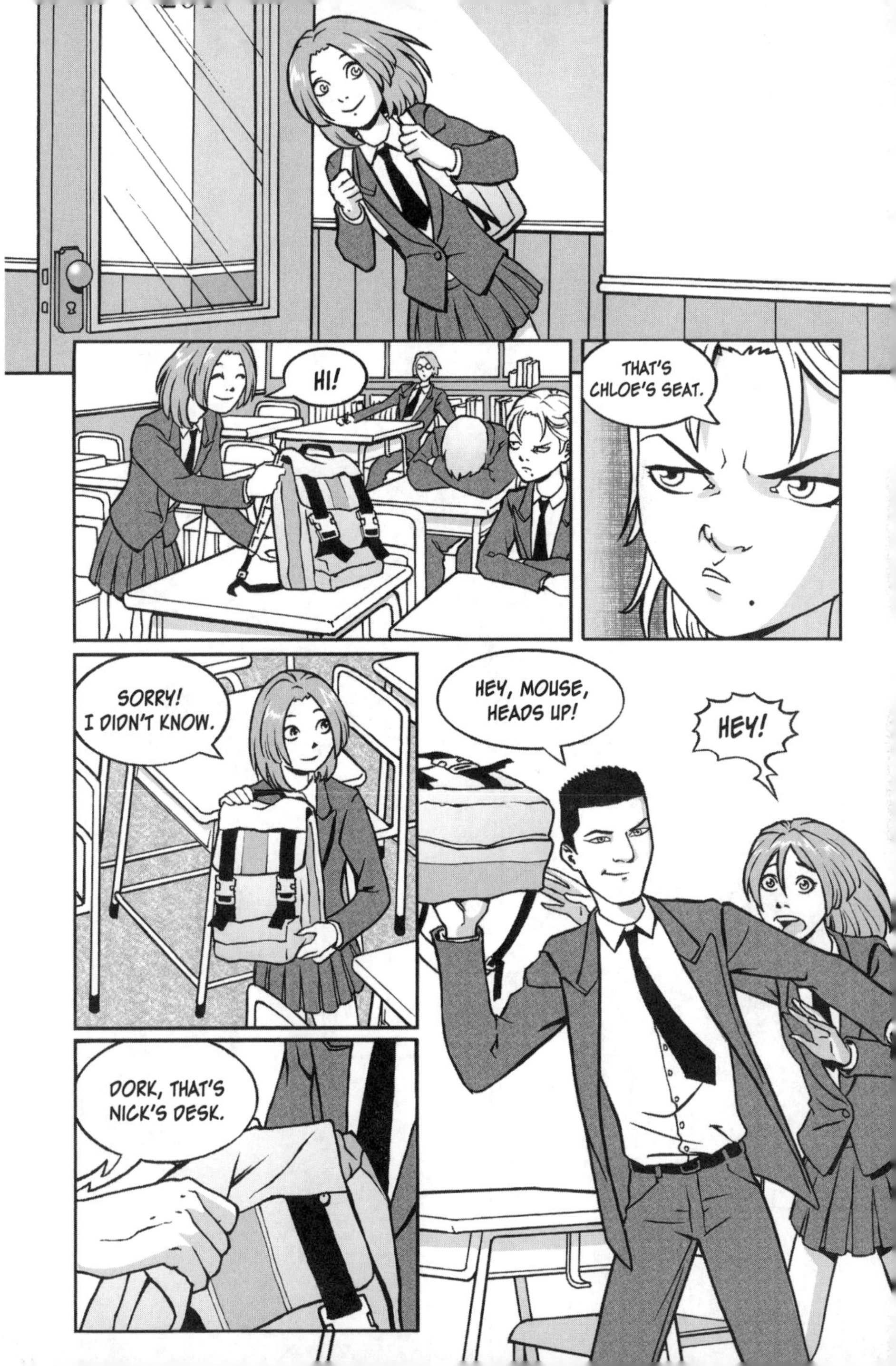
HI!
THAT'S CHLOE'S SEAT.
SORRY! I DIDN'T KNOW.
HEY, MOUSE, HEADS UP!
HEY!
DORK, THAT'S NICK'S DESK.

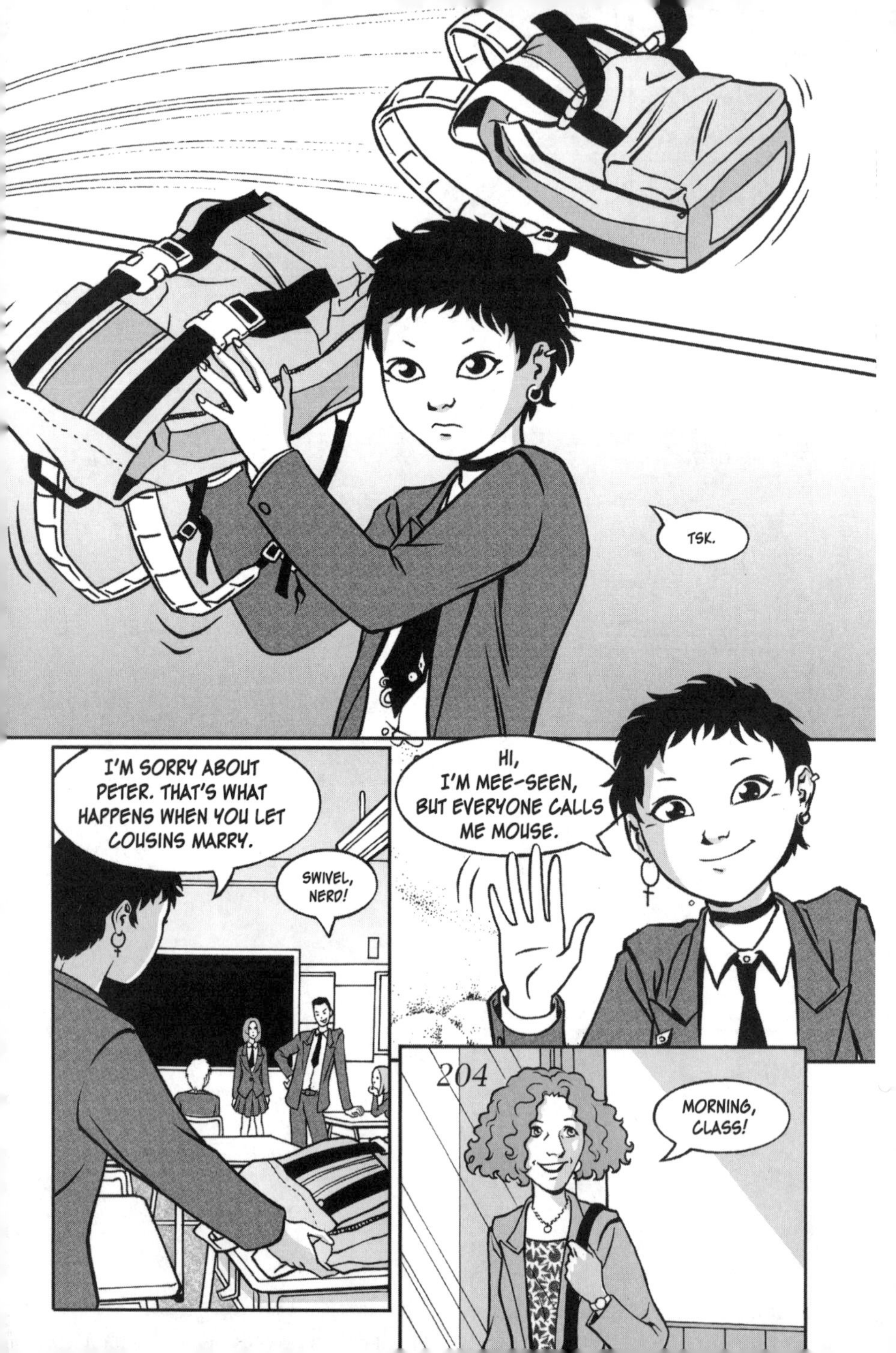
TSK.
I'M SORRY ABOUT PETER. THAT'S WHAT HAPPENS WHEN YOU LET COUSINS MARRY.
SWIVEL, NERD!
HI, I'M MEE-SEEN, BUT EVERYONE CALLS ME MOUSE.
MORNING, CLASS!

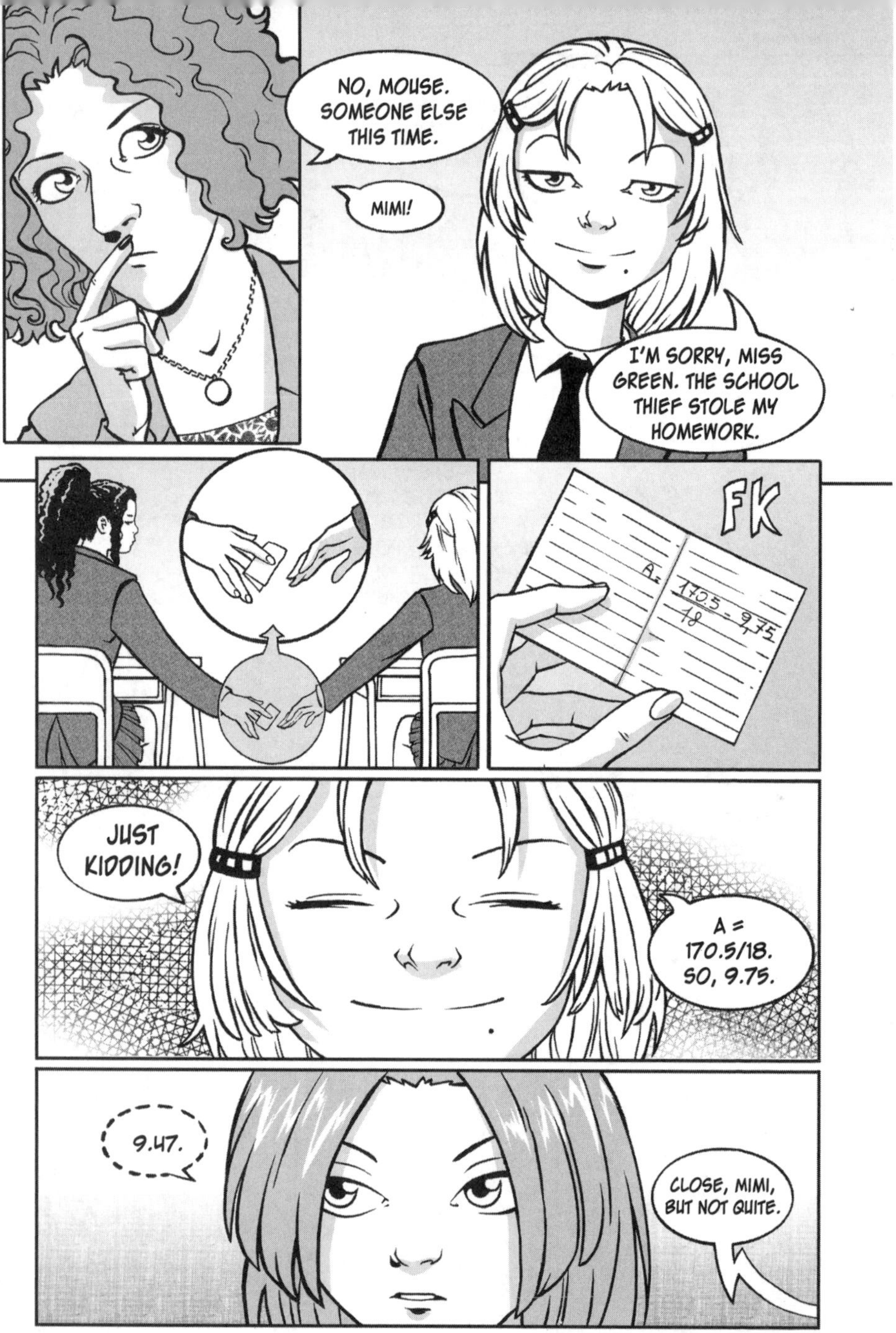
NO, MOUSE. SOMEONE ELSE THIS TIME.
MIMI!
I'M SORRY, MISS GREEN. THE SCHOOL THIEF STOLE MY HOMEWORK.
FK
JUST KIDDING!
A = 170.5/18. SO, 9.75.
9.47.
CLOSE, MIMI, BUT NOT QUITE.

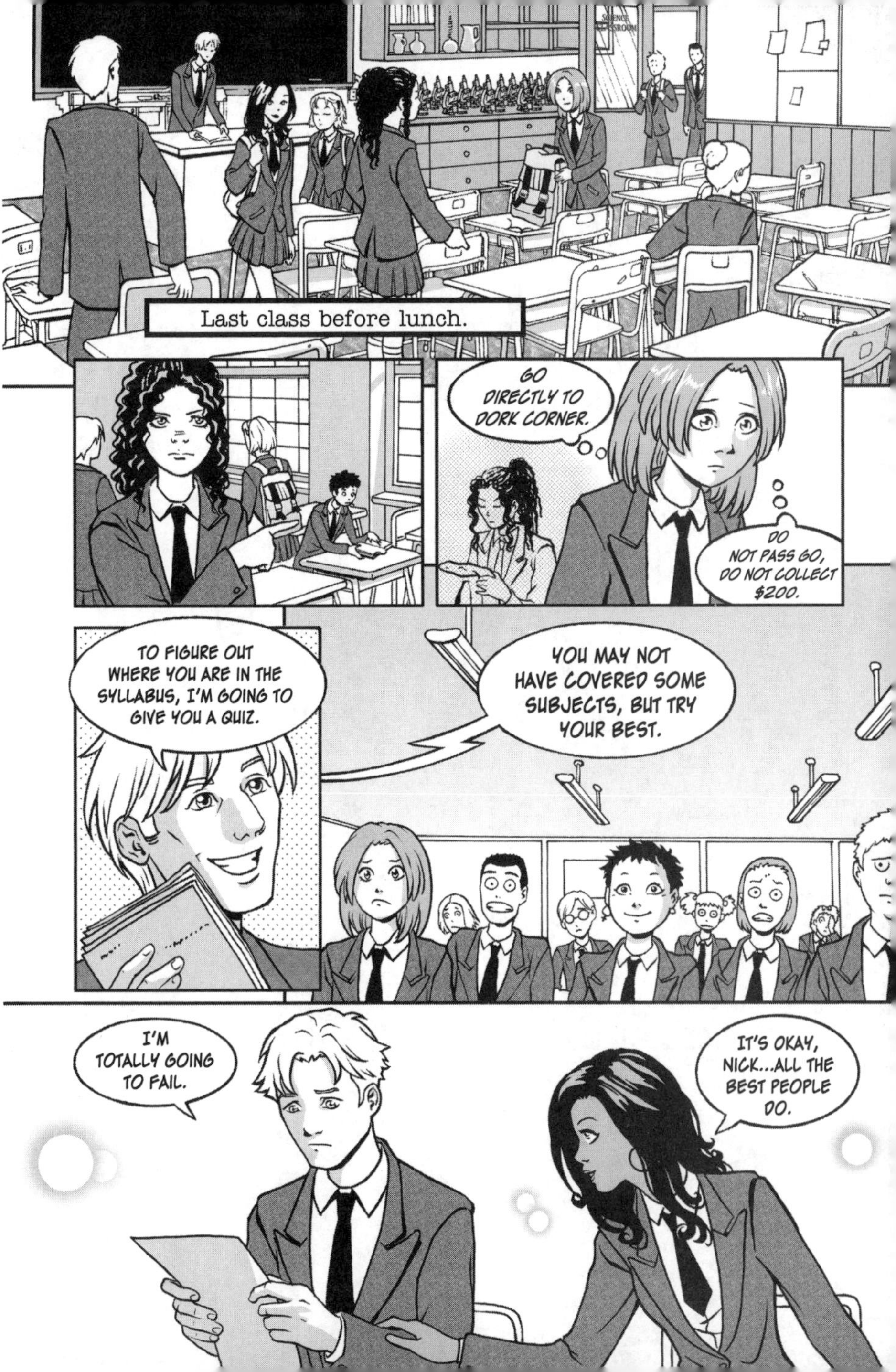
SCIENCE CLASSROOM
Last class before lunch.
GO DIRECTLY TO DORK CORNER.
DO NOT PASS GO, DO NOT COLLECT $200.
TO FIGURE OUT WHERE YOU ARE IN THE SYLLABUS, I'M GOING TO GIVE YOU A QUIZ.
YOU MAY NOT HAVE COVERED SOME SUBJECTS, BUT TRY YOUR BEST.
I'M TOTALLY GOING TO FAIL.
IT'S OKAY, NICK...ALL THE BEST PEOPLE DO.

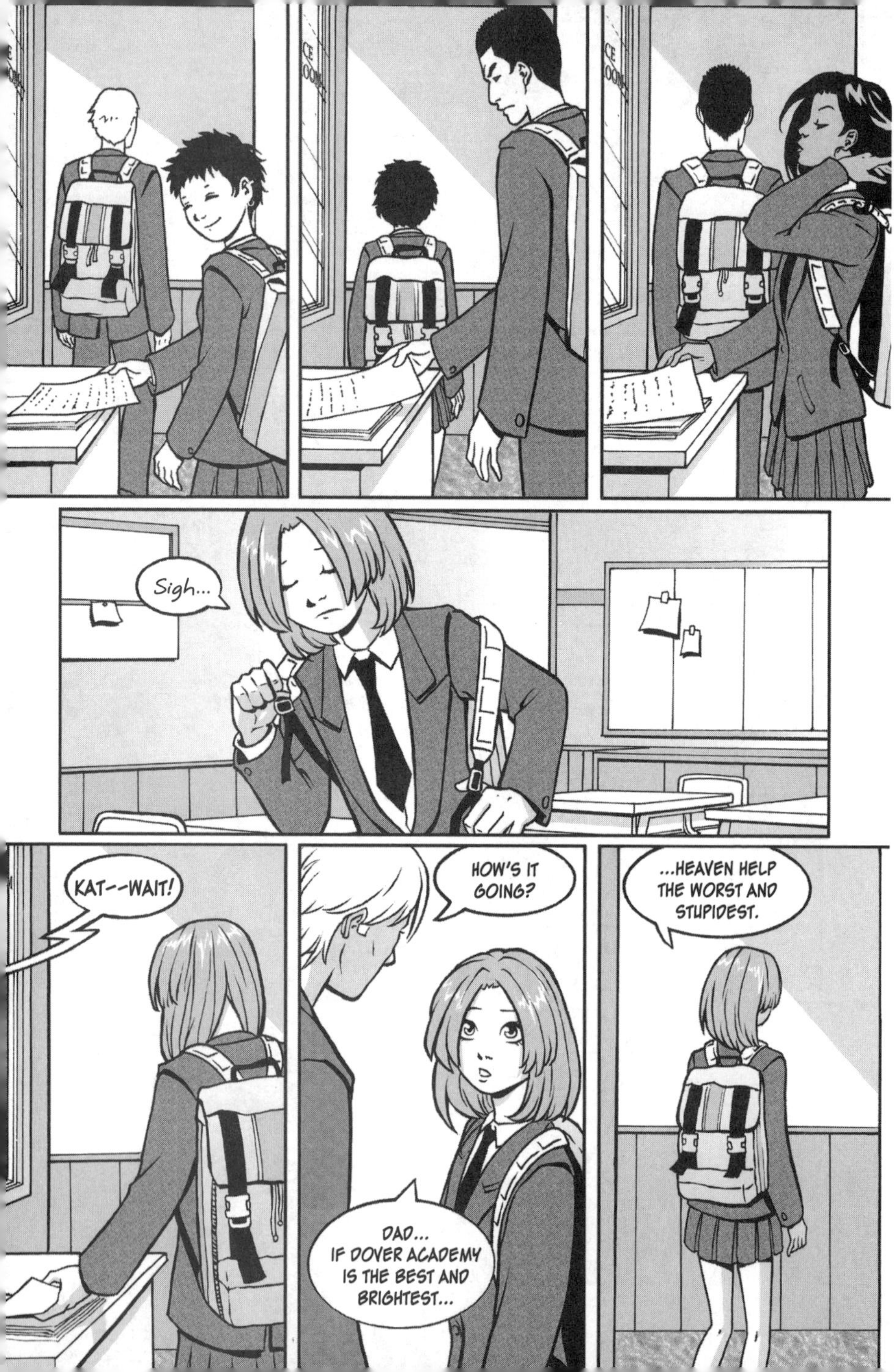
Sigh...
KAT--WAIT!
HOW'S IT GOING?
DAD... IF DOVER ACADEMY IS THE BEST AND BRIGHTEST...
...HEAVEN HELP THE WORST AND STUPIDEST.

# Chapter 2:
# Student Criminals

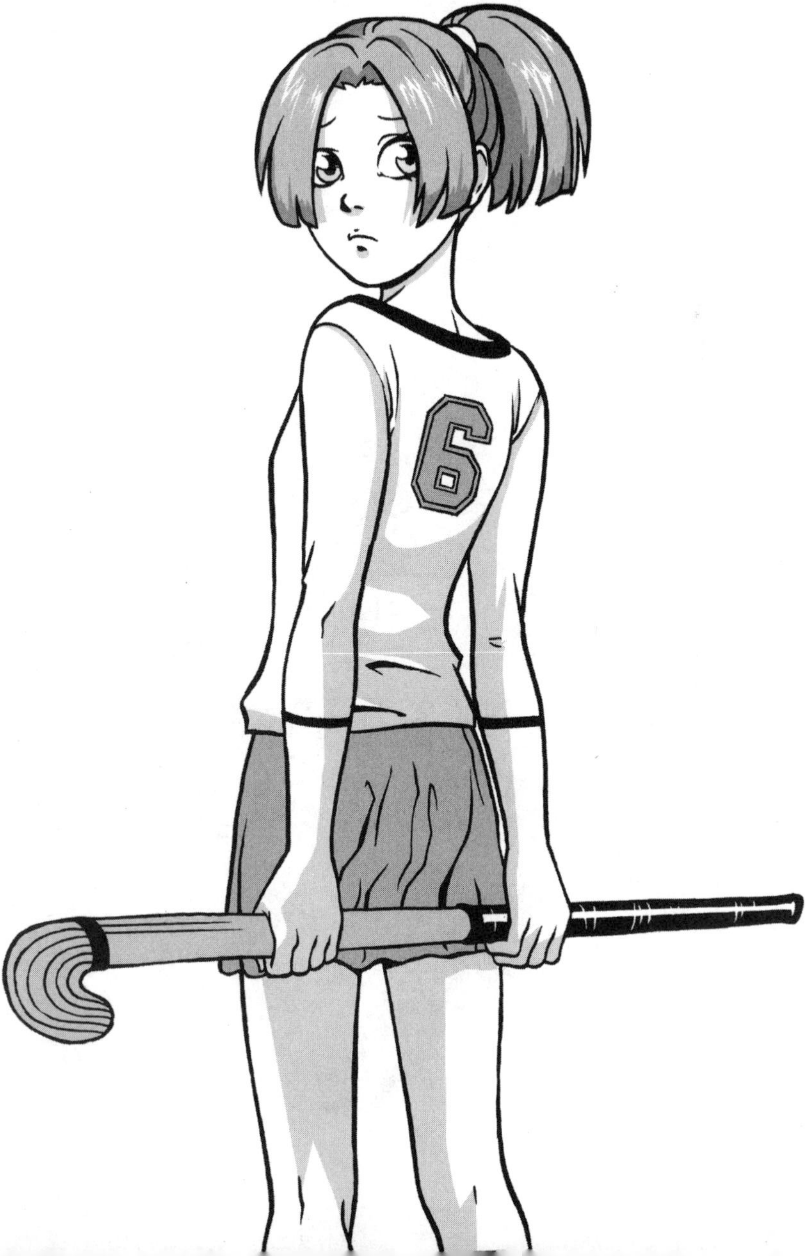

6

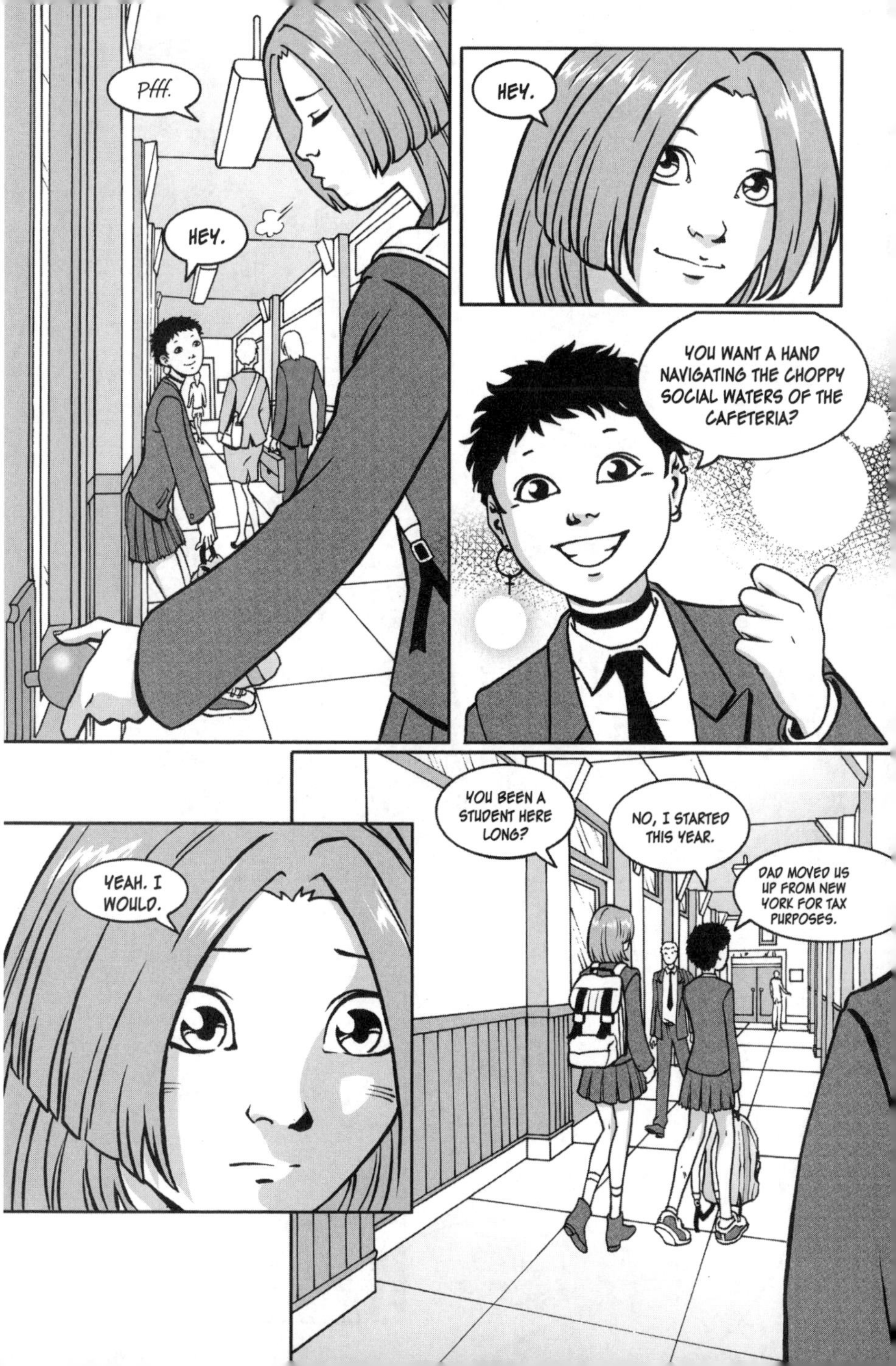
PFFF.
HEY.
HEY.
YOU WANT A HAND NAVIGATING THE CHOPPY SOCIAL WATERS OF THE CAFETERIA?
YEAH. I WOULD.
YOU BEEN A STUDENT HERE LONG?
NO, I STARTED THIS YEAR.
DAD MOVED US UP FROM NEW YORK FOR TAX PURPOSES.

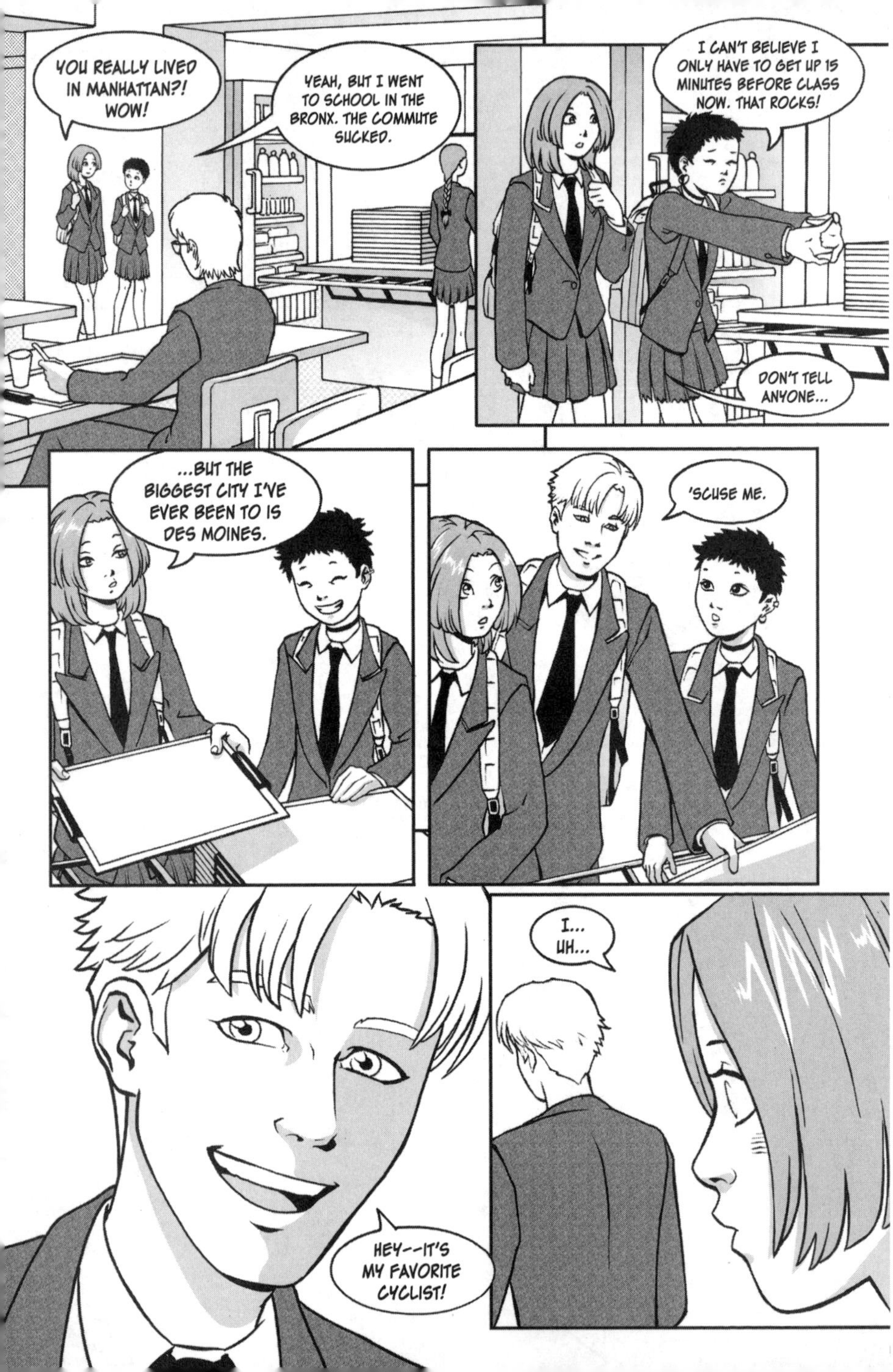
YOU REALLY LIVED IN MANHATTAN?! WOW!
YEAH, BUT I WENT TO SCHOOL IN THE BRONX. THE COMMUTE SUCKED.
I CAN'T BELIEVE I ONLY HAVE TO GET UP 15 MINUTES BEFORE CLASS NOW. THAT ROCKS!
DON'T TELL ANYONE...
...BUT THE BIGGEST CITY I'VE EVER BEEN TO IS DES MOINES.
'SCUSE ME.
HEY--IT'S MY FAVORITE CYCLIST!
I... UH...

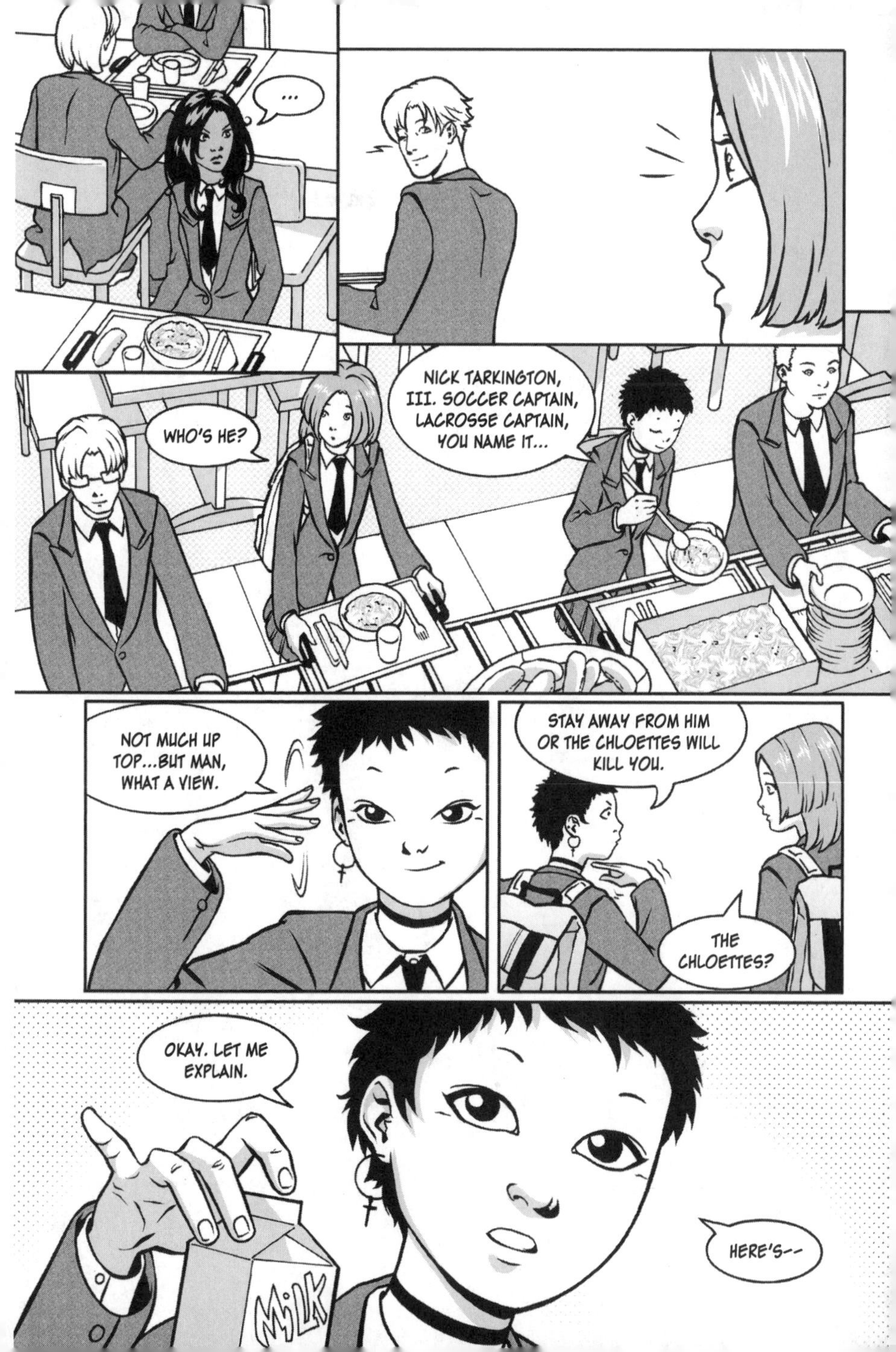
...
WHO'S HE?
NICK TARKINGTON, III. SOCCER CAPTAIN, LACROSSE CAPTAIN, YOU NAME IT...
NOT MUCH UP TOP...BUT MAN, WHAT A VIEW.
STAY AWAY FROM HIM OR THE CHLOETTES WILL KILL YOU.
THE CHLOETTES?
OKAY. LET ME EXPLAIN.
HERE'S--
MILK

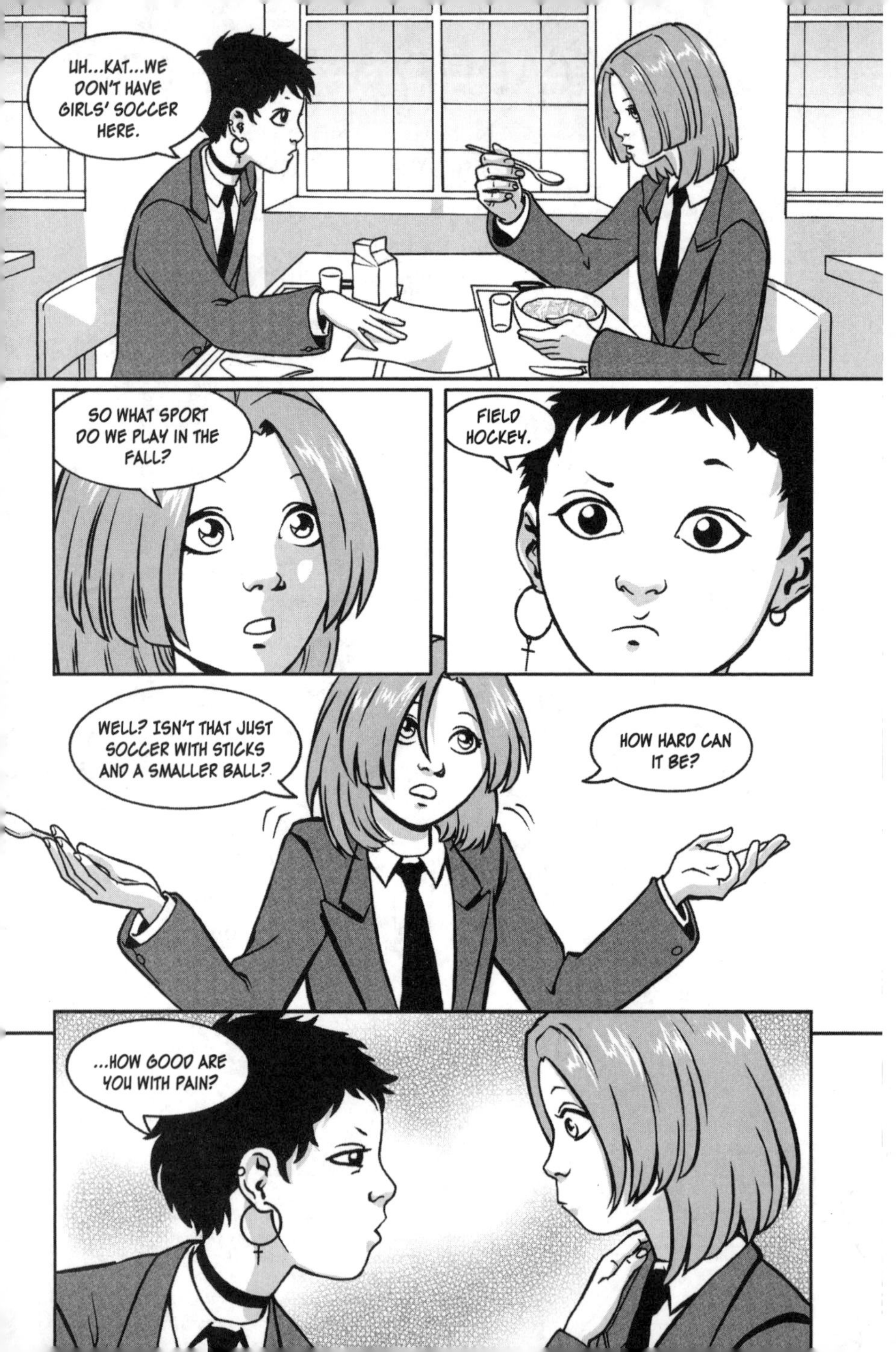
UH...KAT...WE DON'T HAVE GIRLS' SOCCER HERE.
SO WHAT SPORT DO WE PLAY IN THE FALL?
FIELD HOCKEY.
WELL? ISN'T THAT JUST SOCCER WITH STICKS AND A SMALLER BALL?
HOW HARD CAN IT BE?
...HOW GOOD ARE YOU WITH PAIN?

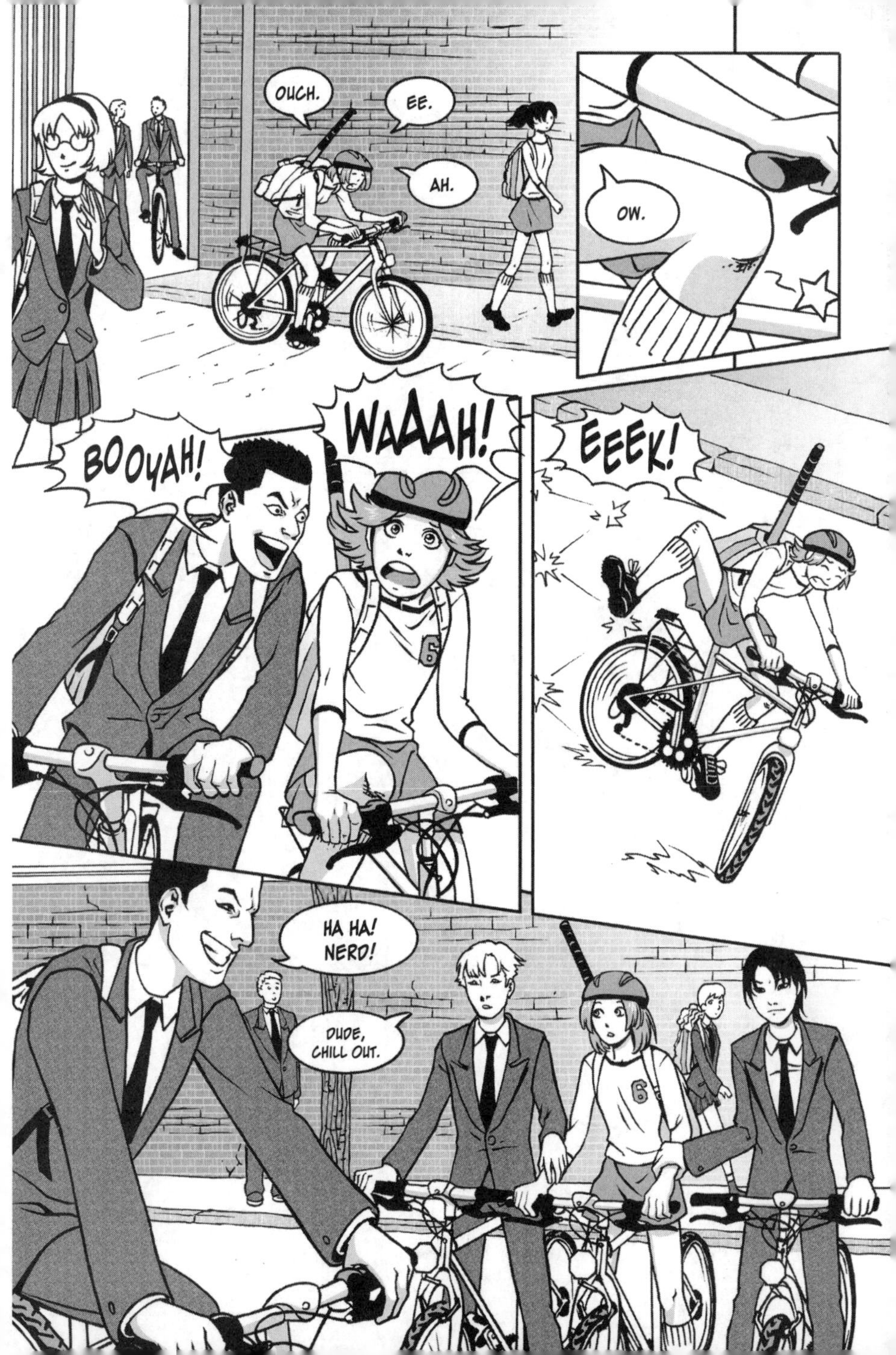
OUCH.
EE.
AH.
OW.
BOOYAH!
WAAAH!
EEEK!
HA HA! NERD!
DUDE, CHILL OUT.

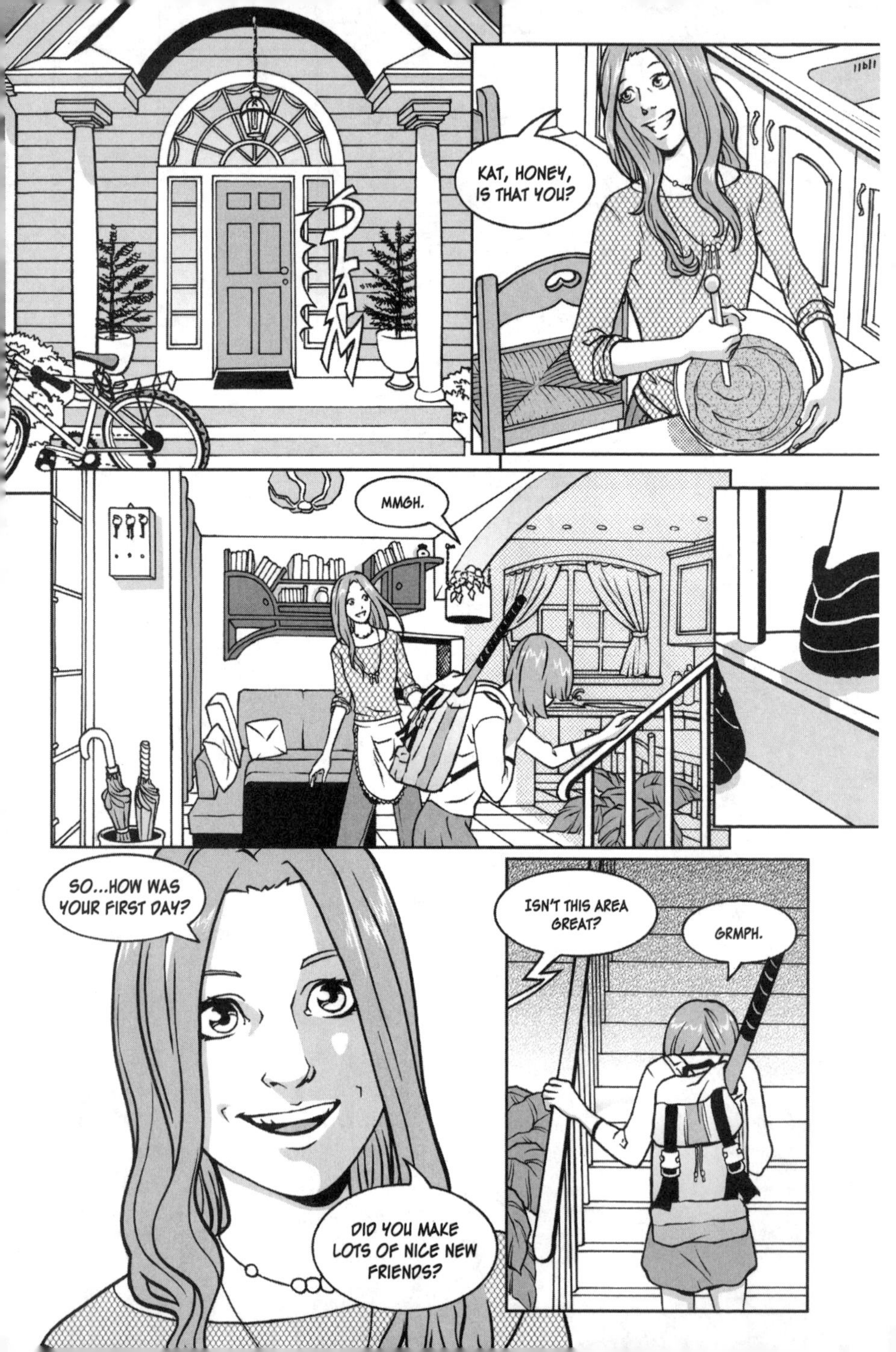
SLAM
KAT, HONEY, IS THAT YOU?
MMGH.
SO...HOW WAS YOUR FIRST DAY?
DID YOU MAKE LOTS OF NICE NEW FRIENDS?
ISN'T THIS AREA GREAT?
GRMPH.

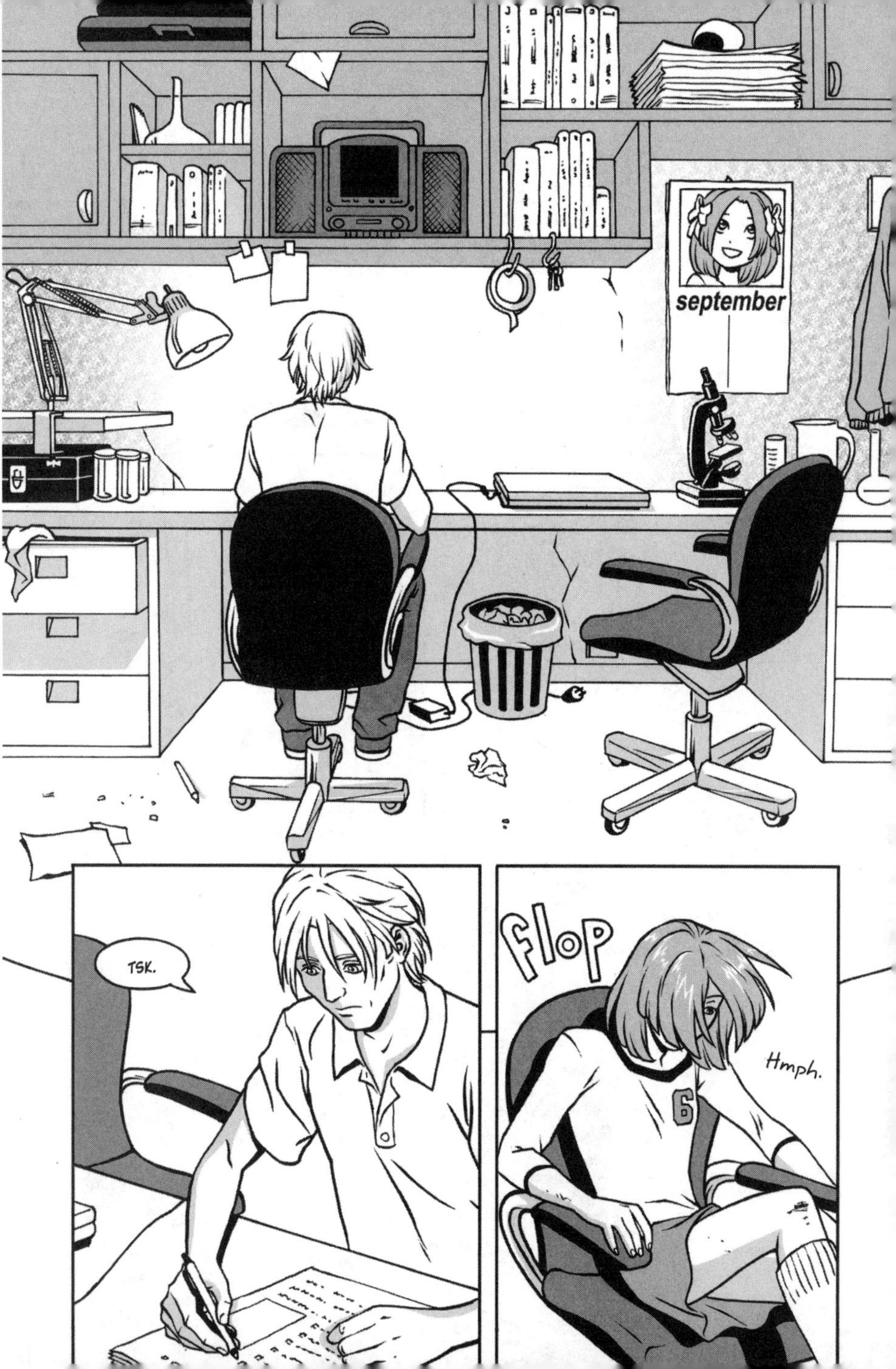
september
TSK.
flop
Hmph.

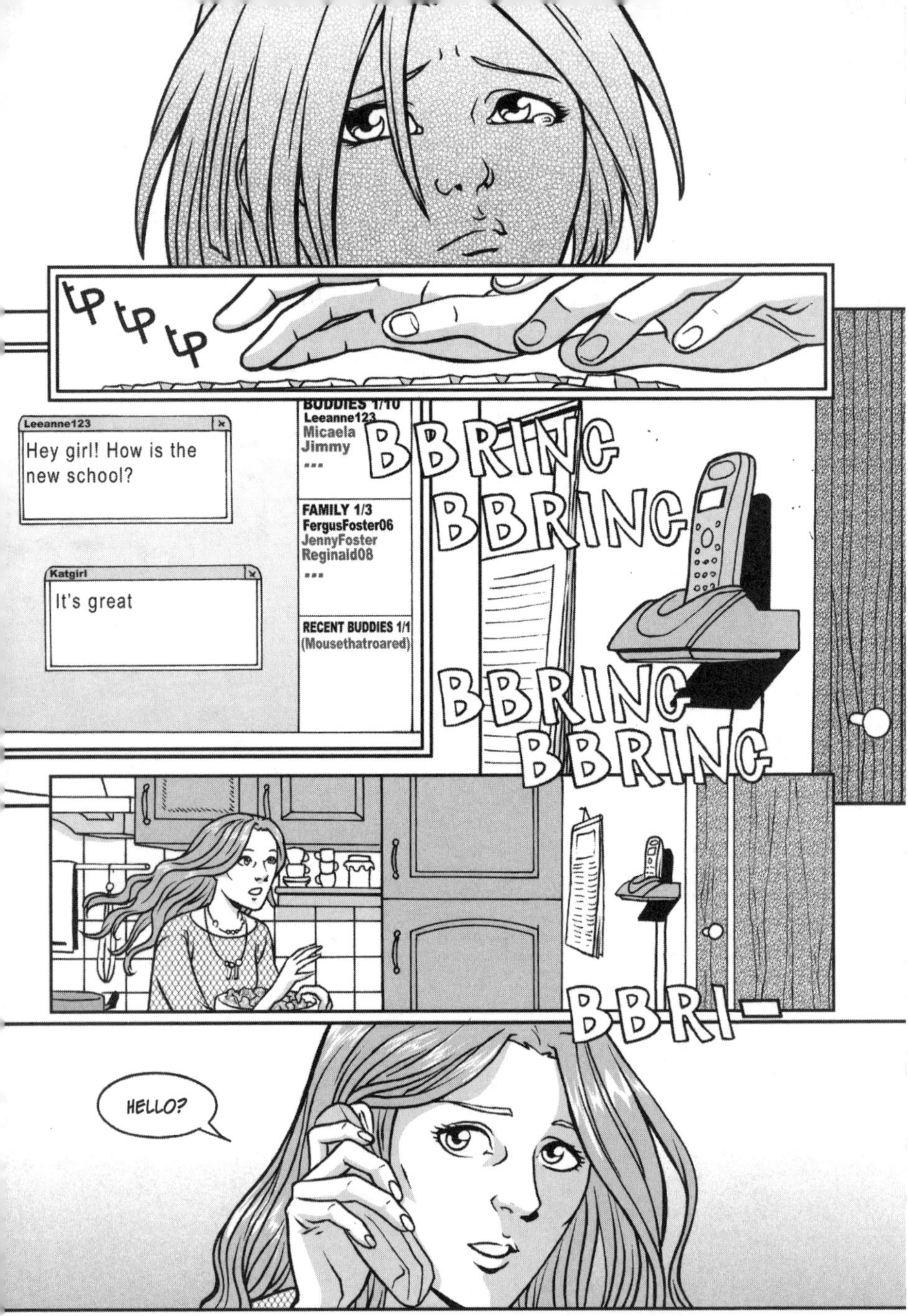
tp tp tp
Leeanne123
Hey girl! How is the new school?
Katgirl
It's great
BUDDIES 1/10
Leeanne123
Micaela
Jimmy
FAMILY 1/3
FergusFoster06
JennyFoster
Reginald08
RECENT BUDDIES 1/1
(Mousethatroared)
BBRING
BBRING
BBRING
BBRING
BBRI-
HELLO?

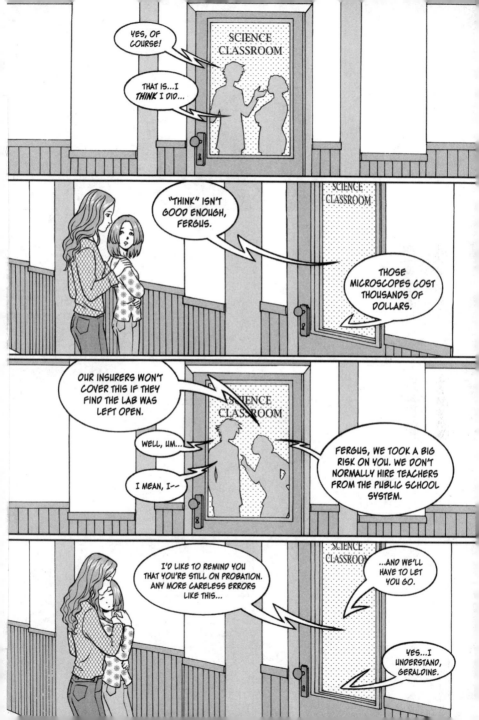

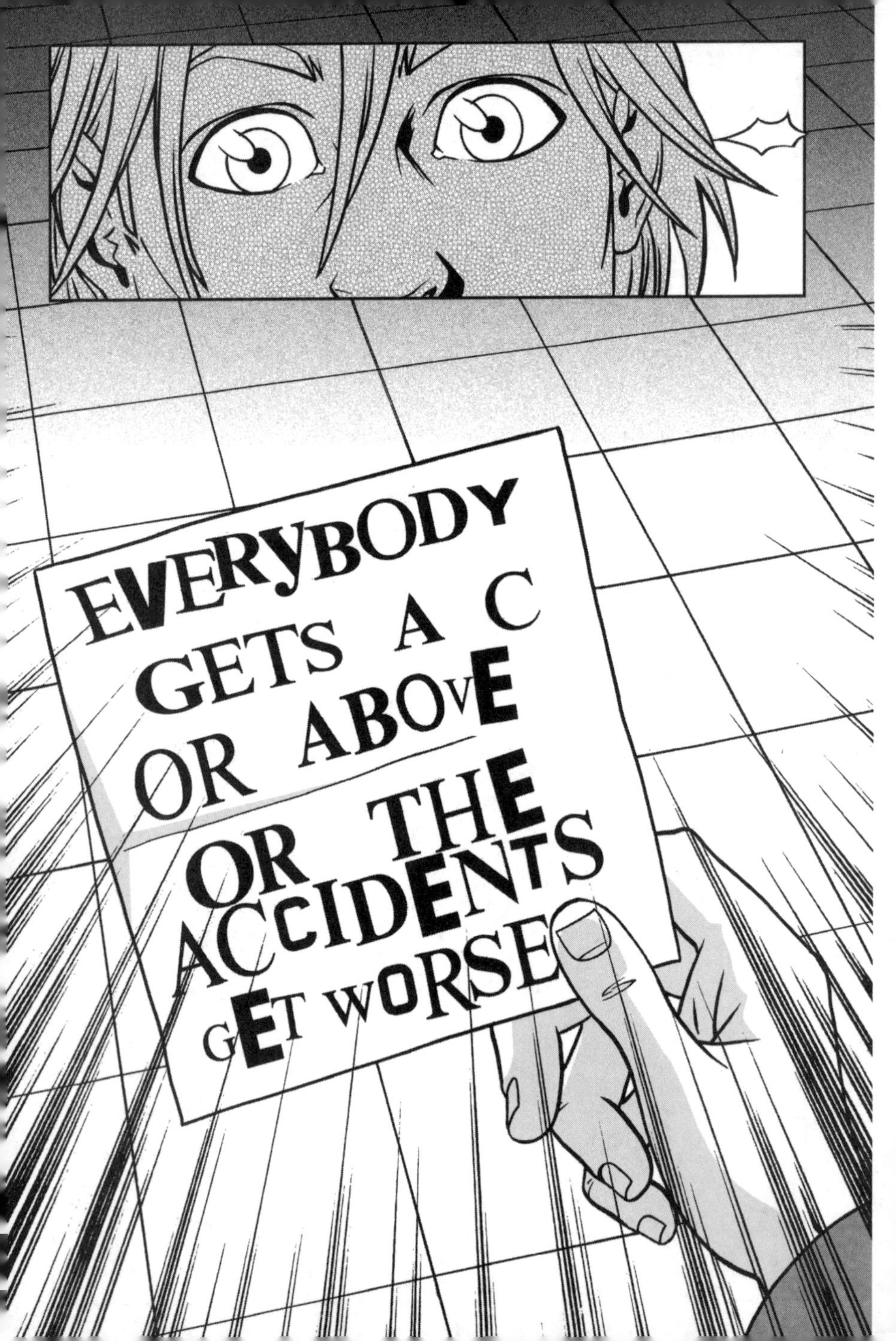
EVERYBODY GETS A C OR ABOVE OR THE ACCIDENTS GET WORSE

# Chapter 3:
# Blackmail

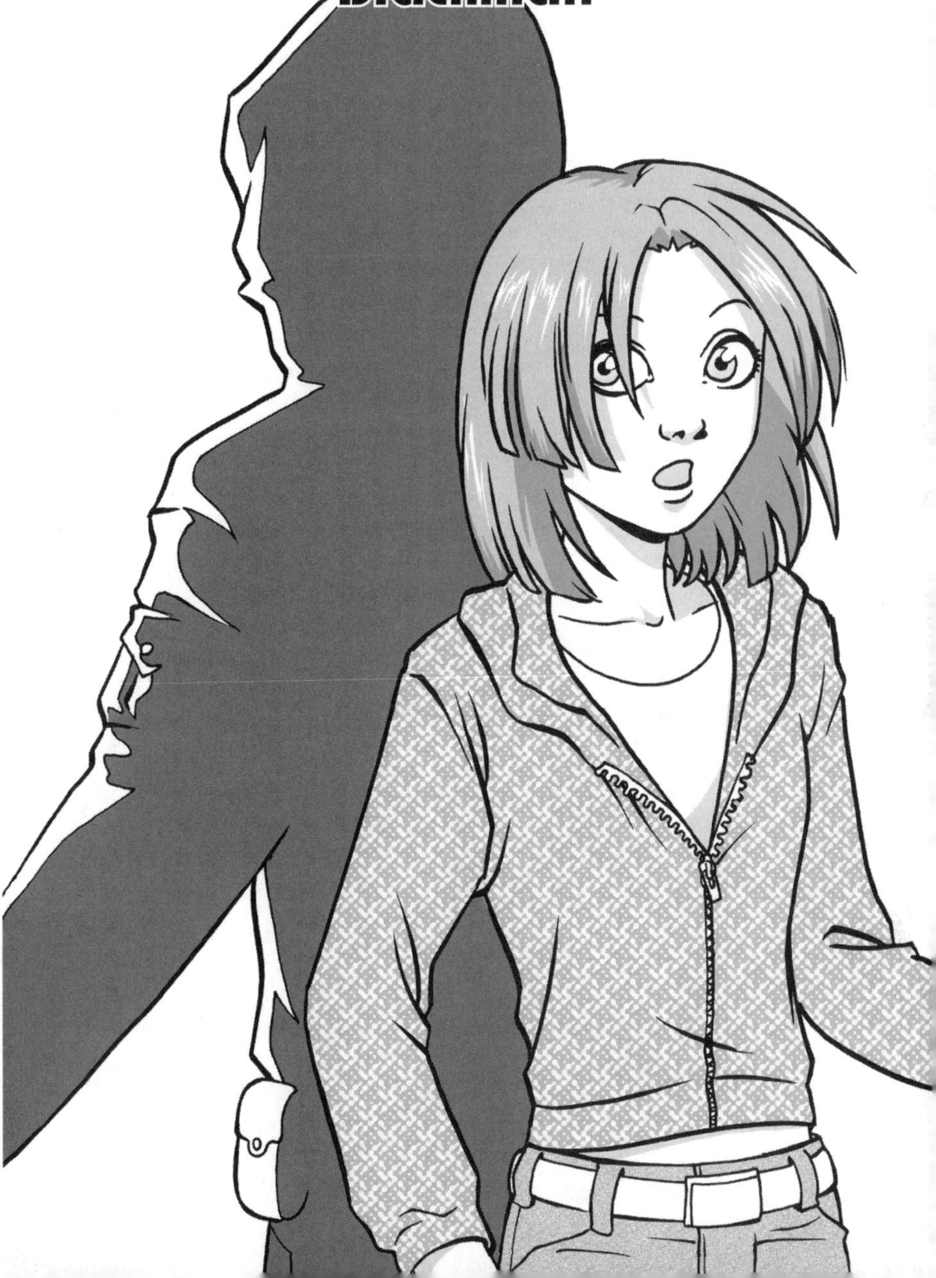

50

51

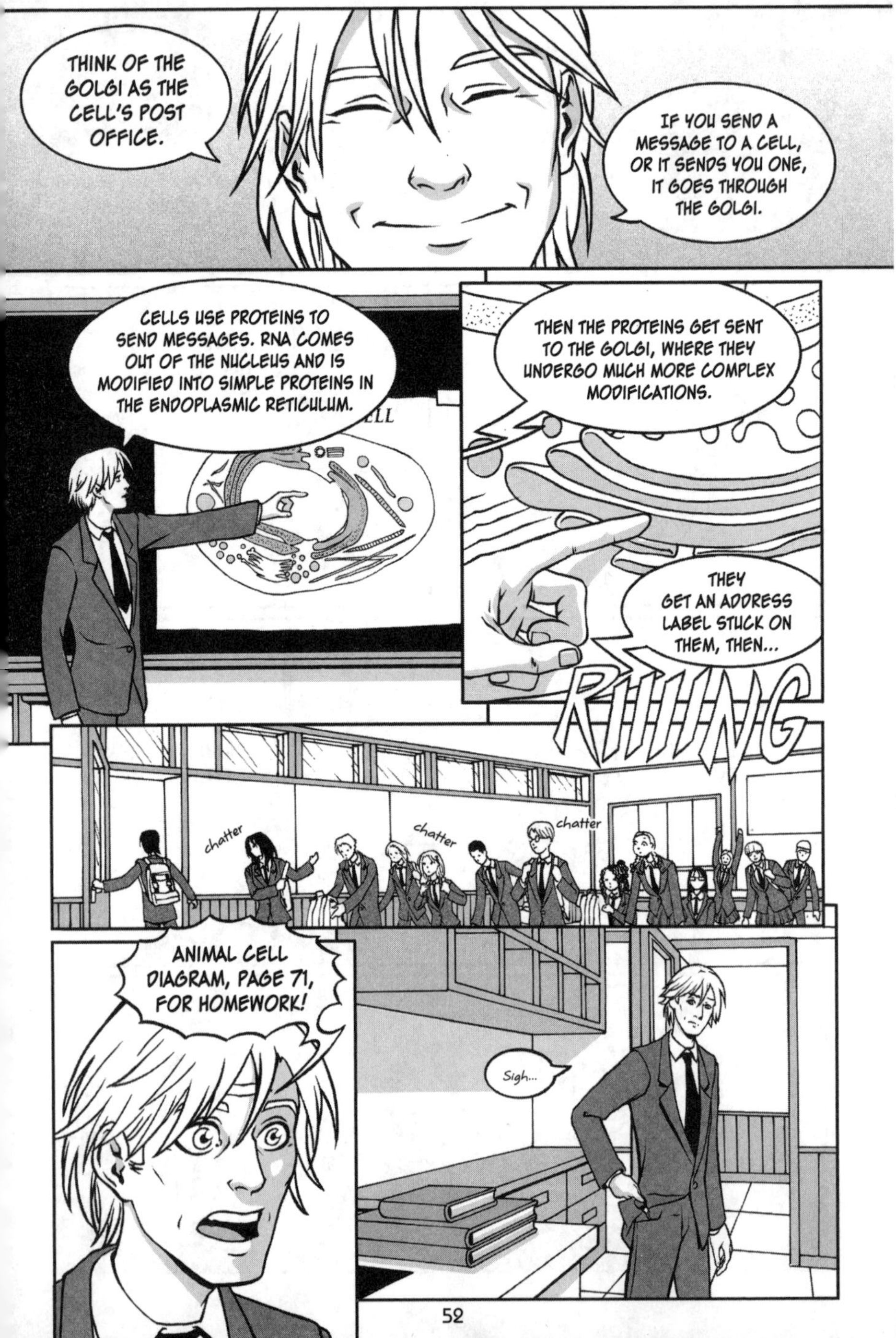
THINK OF THE GOLGI AS THE CELL'S POST OFFICE.
IF YOU SEND A MESSAGE TO A CELL, OR IT SENDS YOU ONE, IT GOES THROUGH THE GOLGI.
CELLS USE PROTEINS TO SEND MESSAGES. RNA COMES OUT OF THE NUCLEUS AND IS MODIFIED INTO SIMPLE PROTEINS IN THE ENDOPLASMIC RETICULUM.
THEN THE PROTEINS GET SENT TO THE GOLGI, WHERE THEY UNDERGO MUCH MORE COMPLEX MODIFICATIONS.
THEY GET AN ADDRESS LABEL STUCK ON THEM, THEN...
RIIING
chatter
chatter
chatter
ANIMAL CELL DIAGRAM, PAGE 71, FOR HOMEWORK!
Sigh...

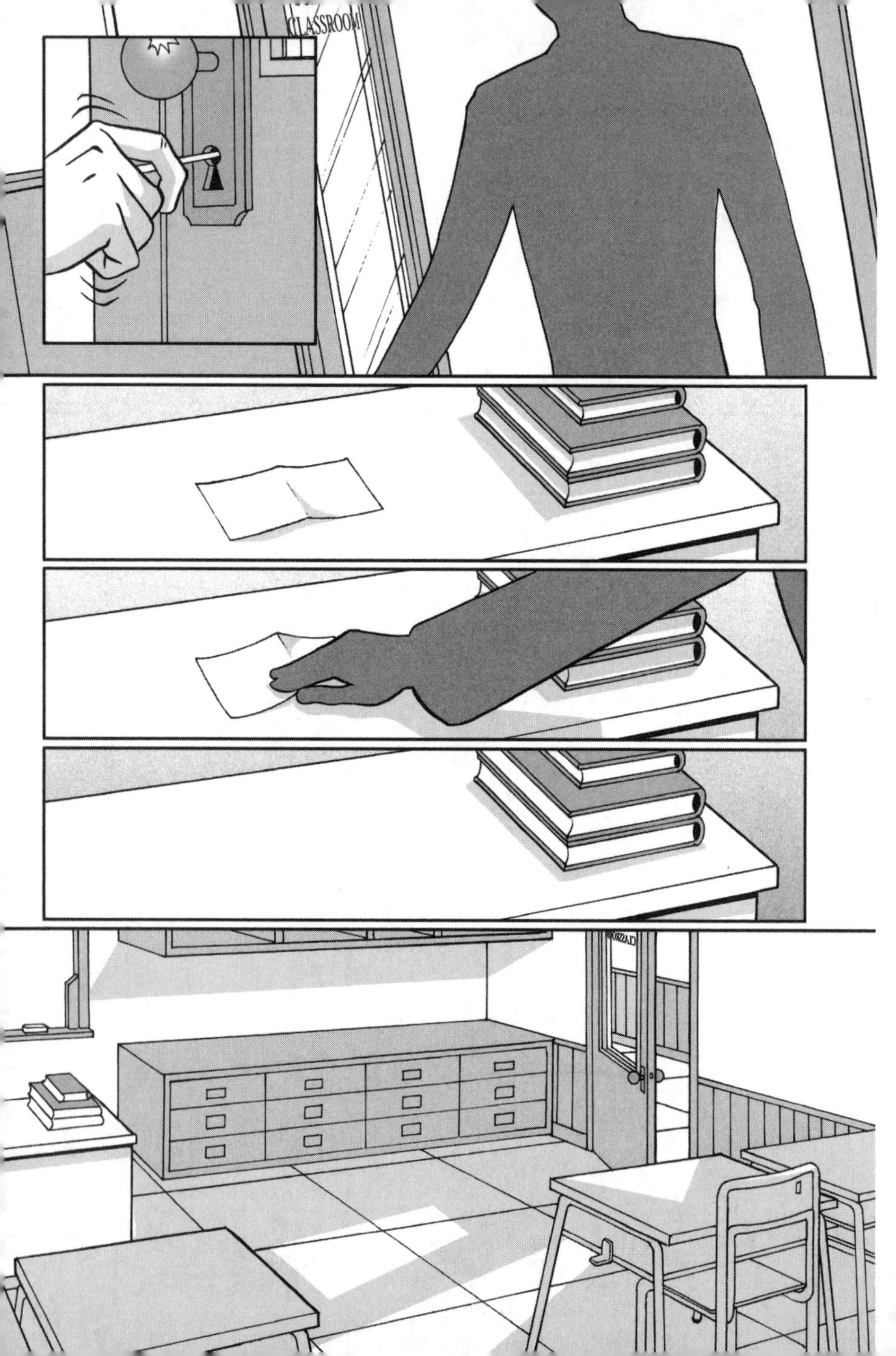
CLASSROOM

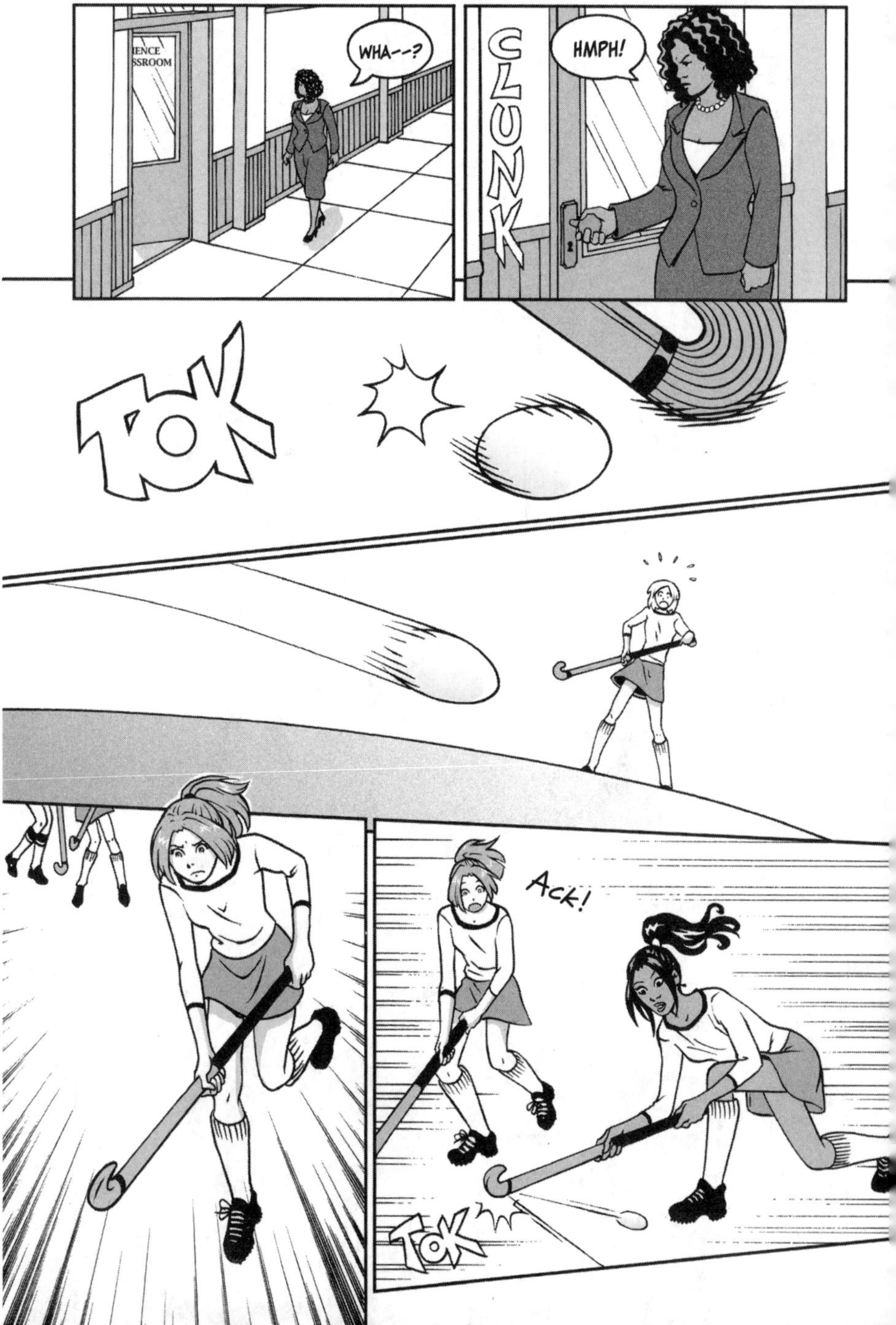
IENCE
SSROOM
WHA--?
HMPH!
CLUNK
TOK
Ack!
TOK

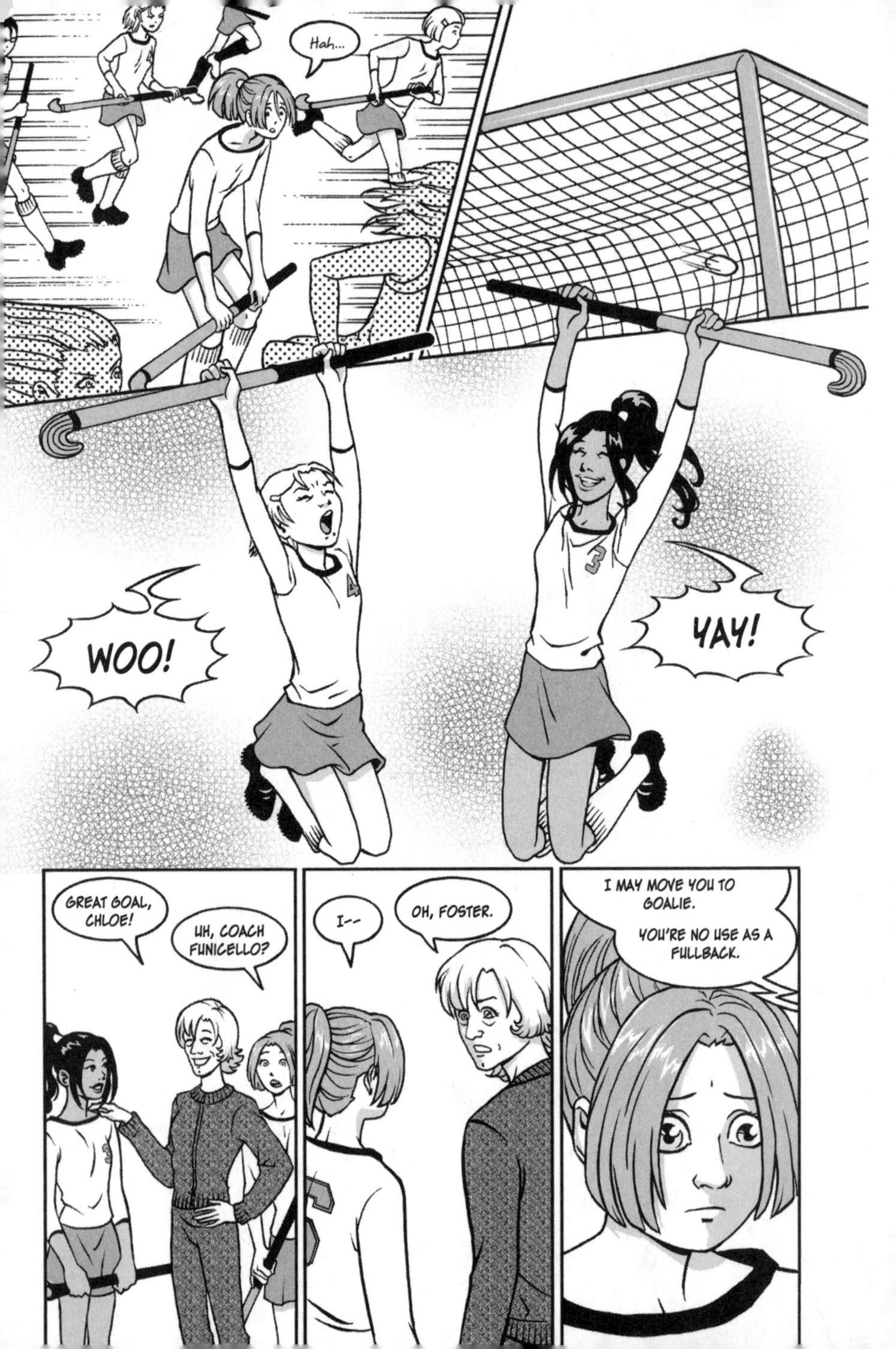
Hah...
WOO!
YAY!
GREAT GOAL, CHLOE!
UH, COACH FUNICELLO?
I--
OH, FOSTER.
I MAY MOVE YOU TO GOALIE.
YOU'RE NO USE AS A FULLBACK.

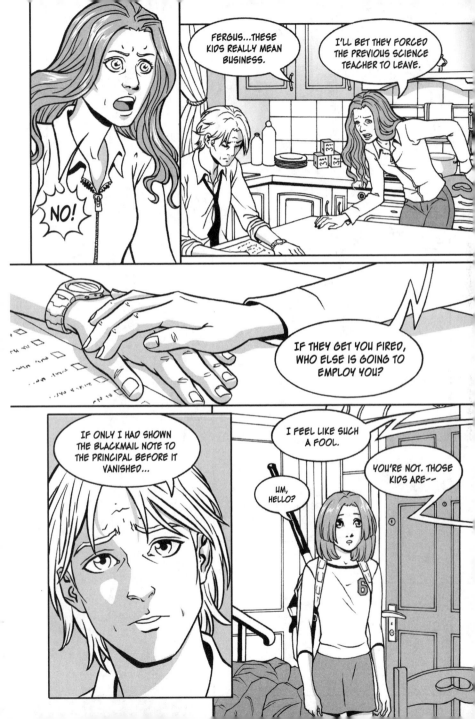

62

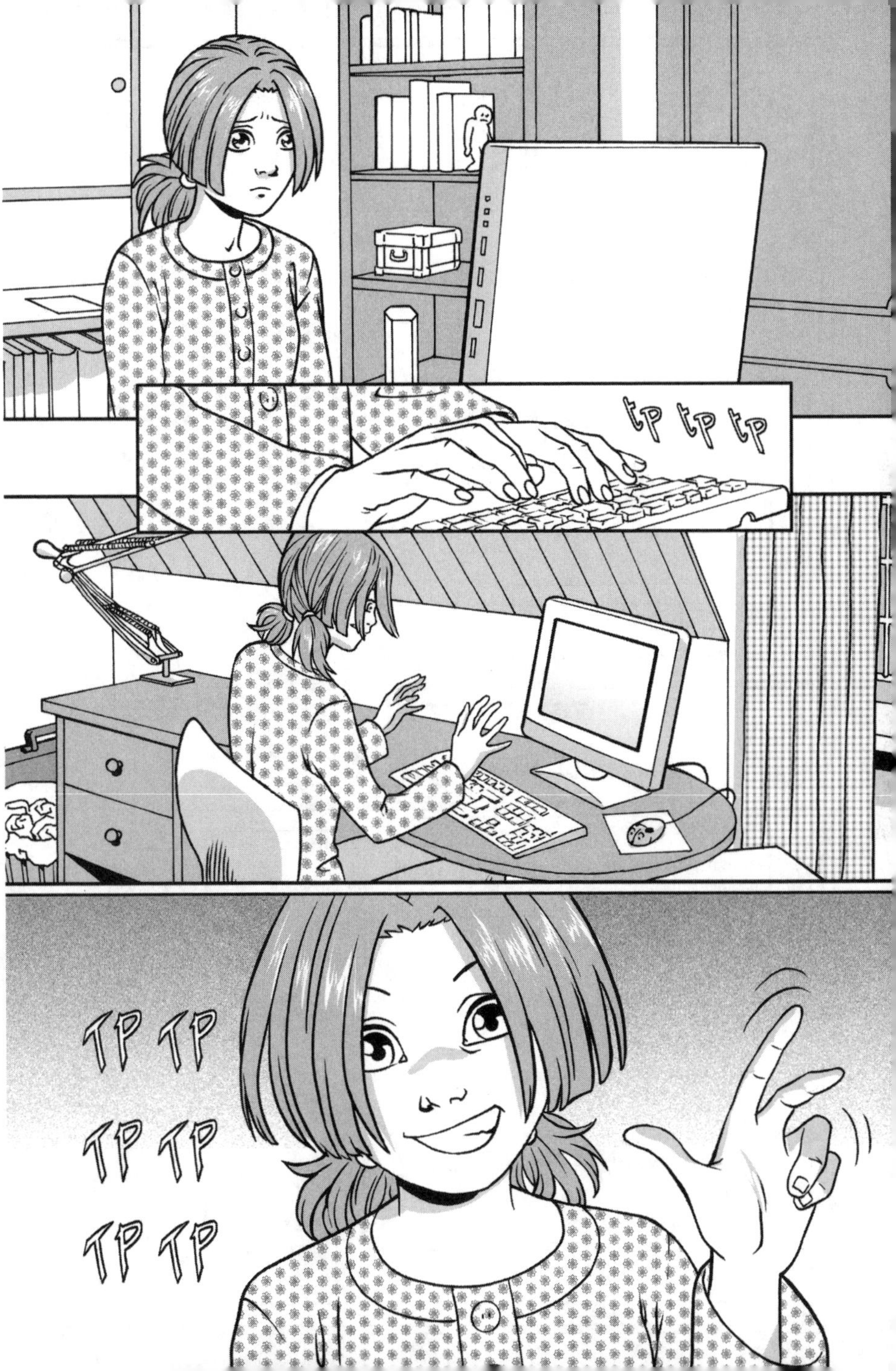
tp tp tp
TP TP
TP TP
TP TP

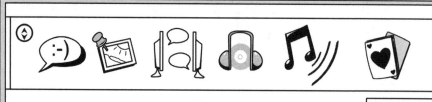

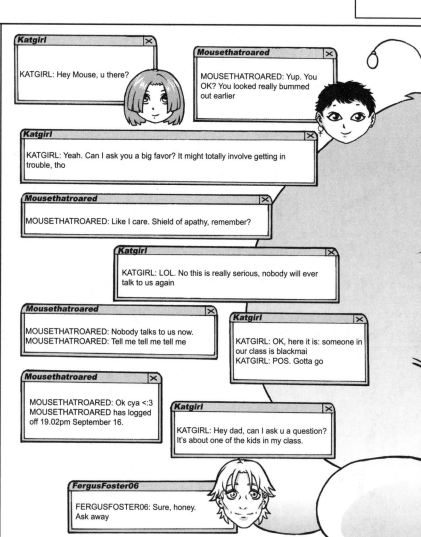

**Katgirl**

KATGIRL: Hey Mouse, u there?

**Mousethatroared**

MOUSETHATROARED: Yup. You OK? You looked really bummed out earlier

**Katgirl**

KATGIRL: Yeah. Can I ask you a big favor? It might totally involve getting in trouble, tho

**Mousethatroared**

MOUSETHATROARED: Like I care. Shield of apathy, remember?

**Katgirl**

KATGIRL: LOL. No this is really serious, nobody will ever talk to us again

**Mousethatroared**

MOUSETHATROARED: Nobody talks to us now.
MOUSETHATROARED: Tell me tell me tell me

**Katgirl**

KATGIRL: OK, here it is: someone in our class is blackmai
KATGIRL: POS. Gotta go

**Mousethatroared**

MOUSETHATROARED: Ok cya <:3
MOUSETHATROARED has logged off 19.02pm September 16.

**Katgirl**

KATGIRL: Hey dad, can I ask u a question? It's about one of the kids in my class.

**FergusFoster06**

FERGUSFOSTER06: Sure, honey. Ask away

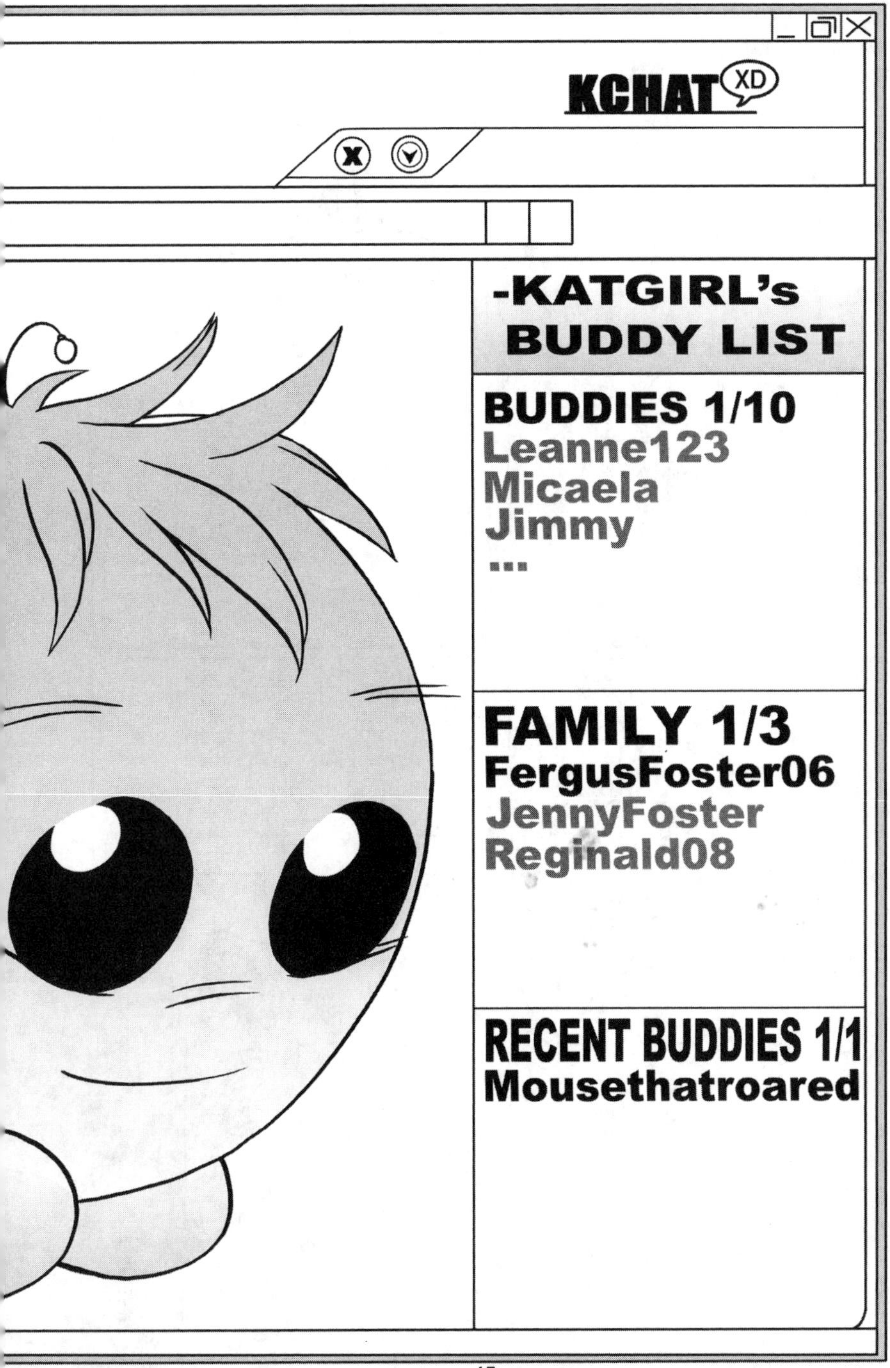
KCHAT XD
-KATGIRL's BUDDY LIST
BUDDIES 1/10
Leanne123
Micaela
Jimmy
...
FAMILY 1/3
FergusFoster06
JennyFoster
Reginald08
RECENT BUDDIES 1/1
Mousethatroared

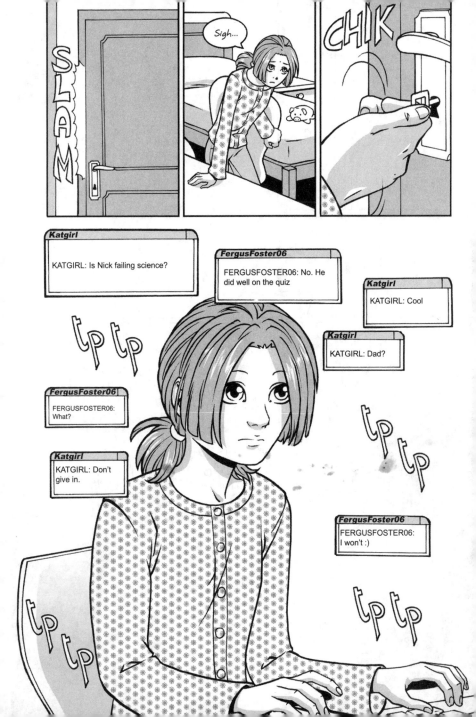

# Chapter 4:
# The Sting

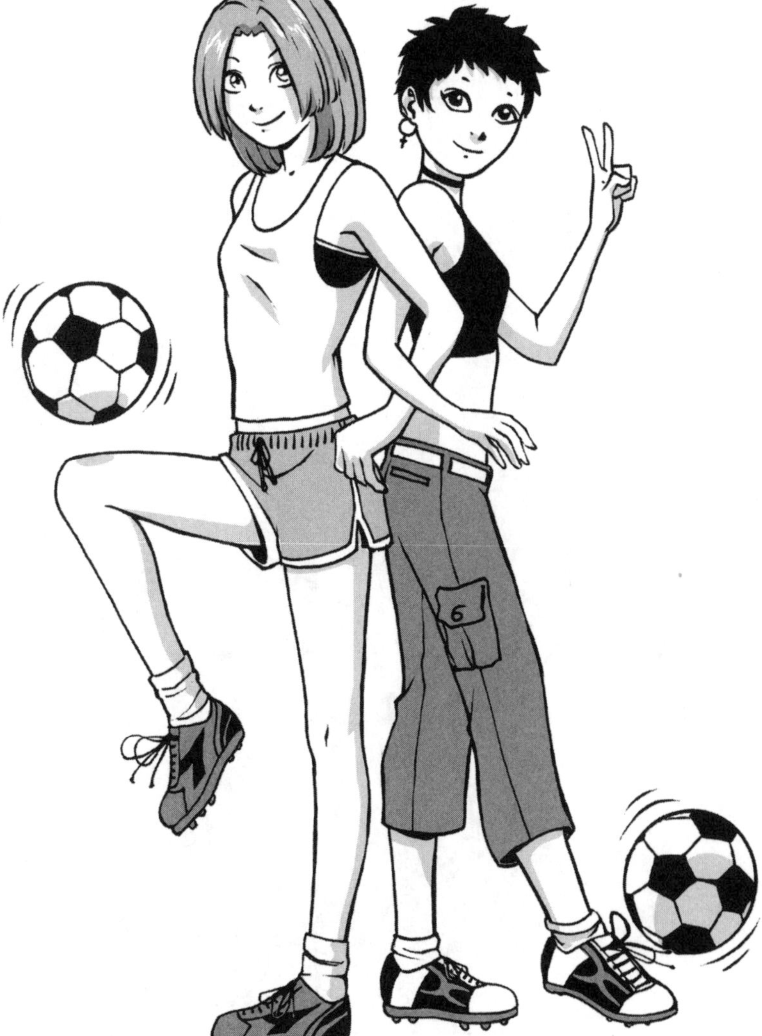
6

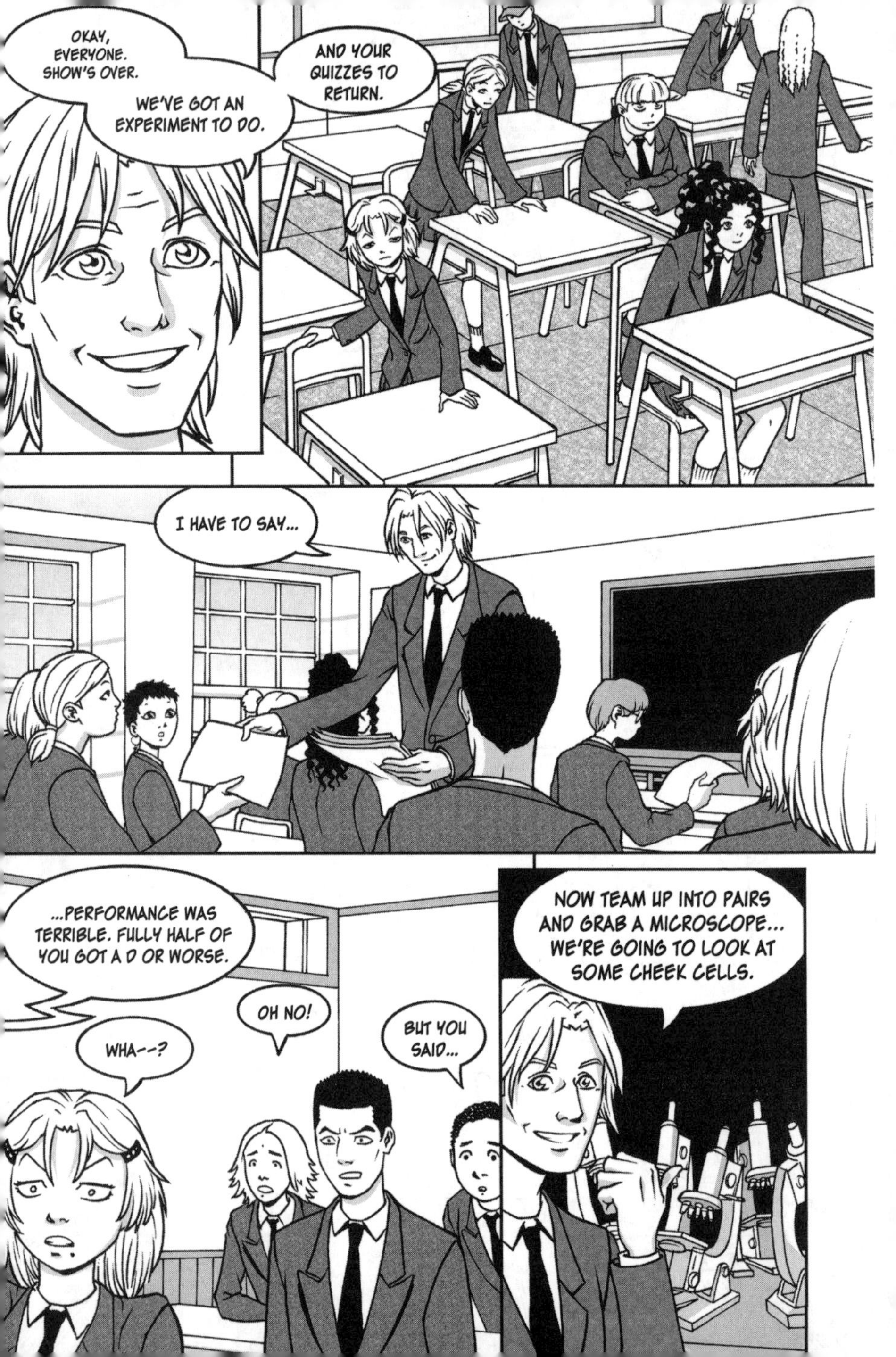
OKAY, EVERYONE. SHOW'S OVER.
WE'VE GOT AN EXPERIMENT TO DO.
AND YOUR QUIZZES TO RETURN.
I HAVE TO SAY...
...PERFORMANCE WAS TERRIBLE. FULLY HALF OF YOU GOT A D OR WORSE.
WHA--?
OH NO!
BUT YOU SAID...
NOW TEAM UP INTO PAIRS AND GRAB A MICROSCOPE... WE'RE GOING TO LOOK AT SOME CHEEK CELLS.

74

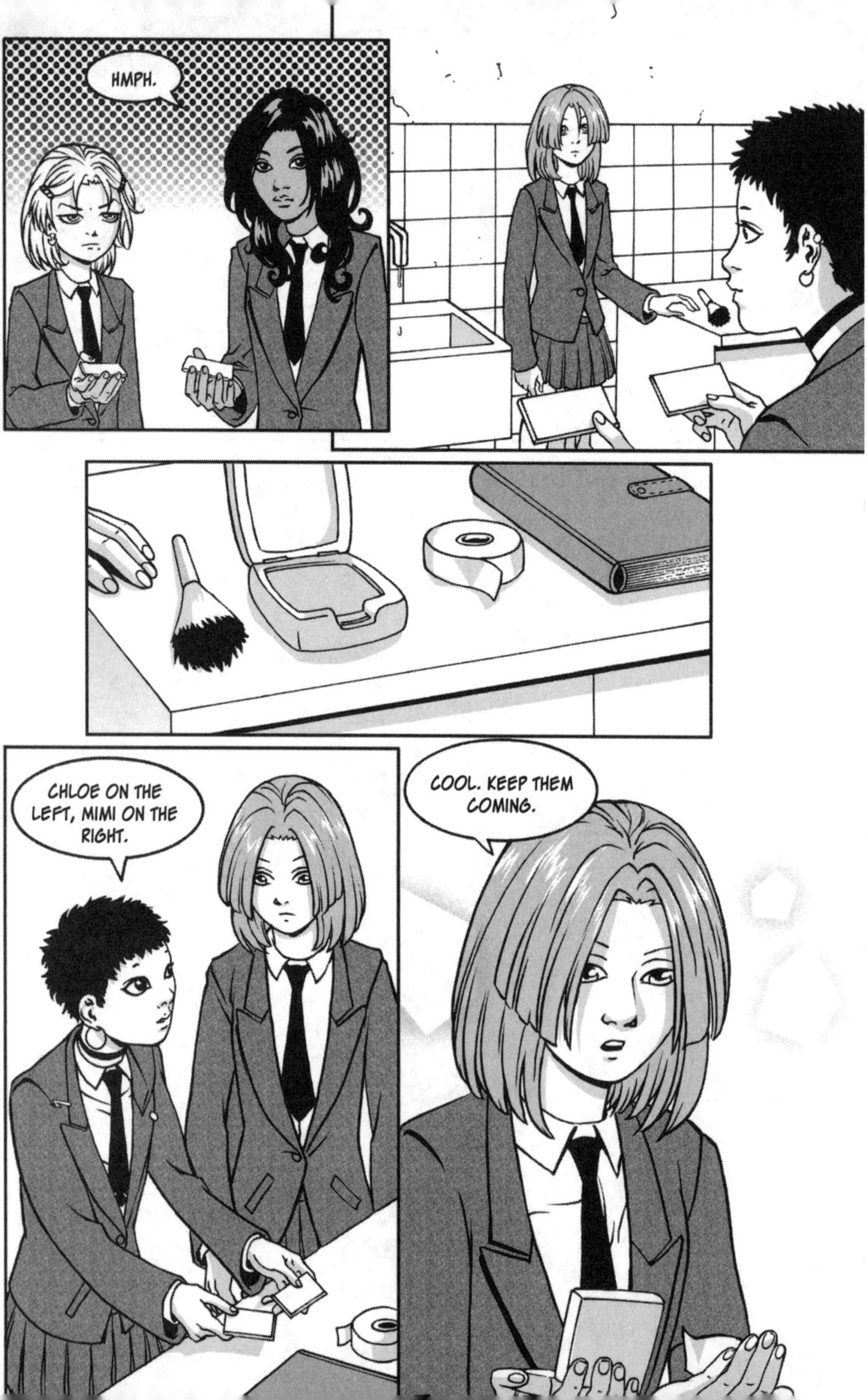
HMPH.
CHLOE ON THE LEFT, MIMI ON THE RIGHT.
COOL. KEEP THEM COMING.

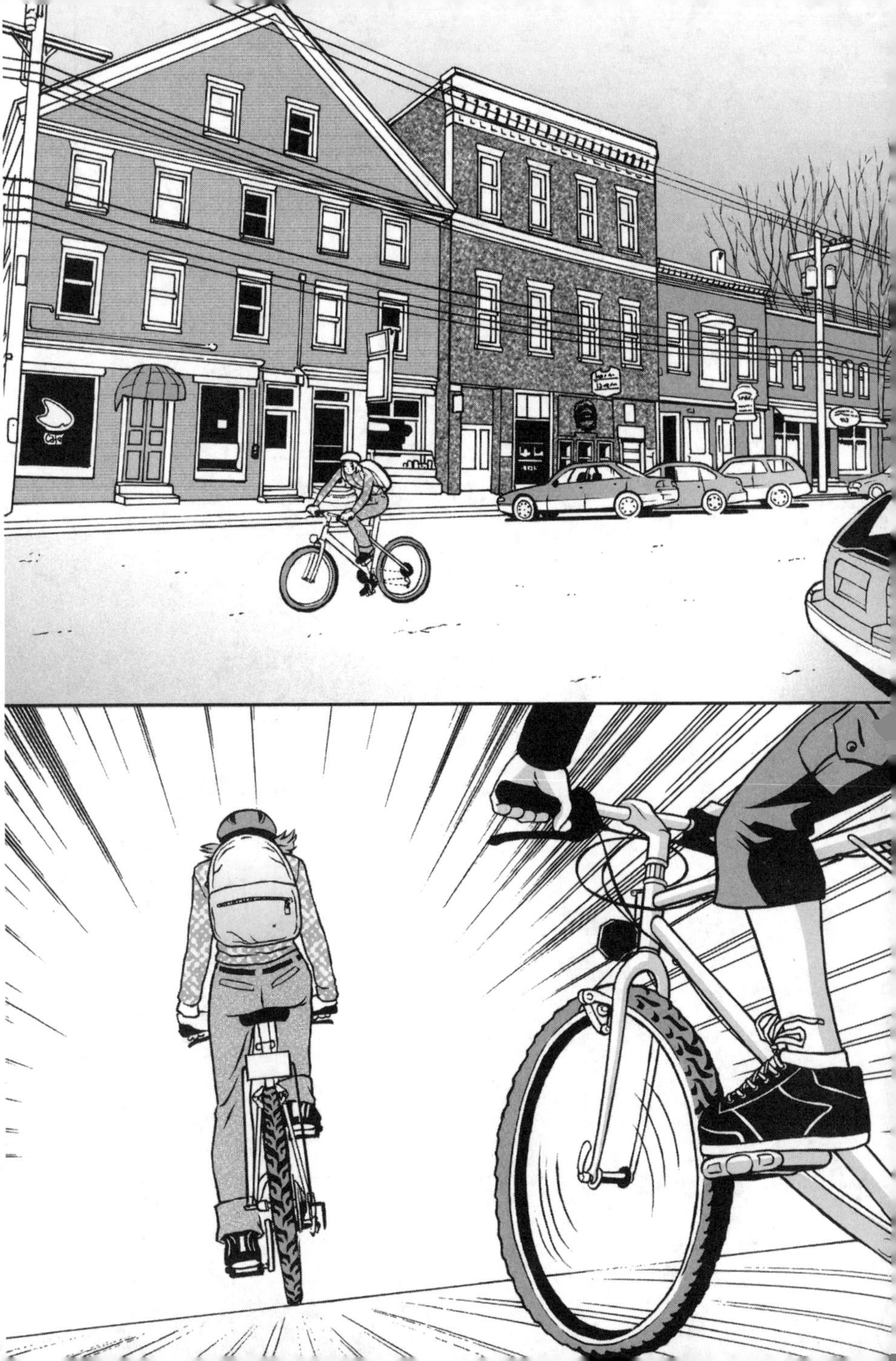

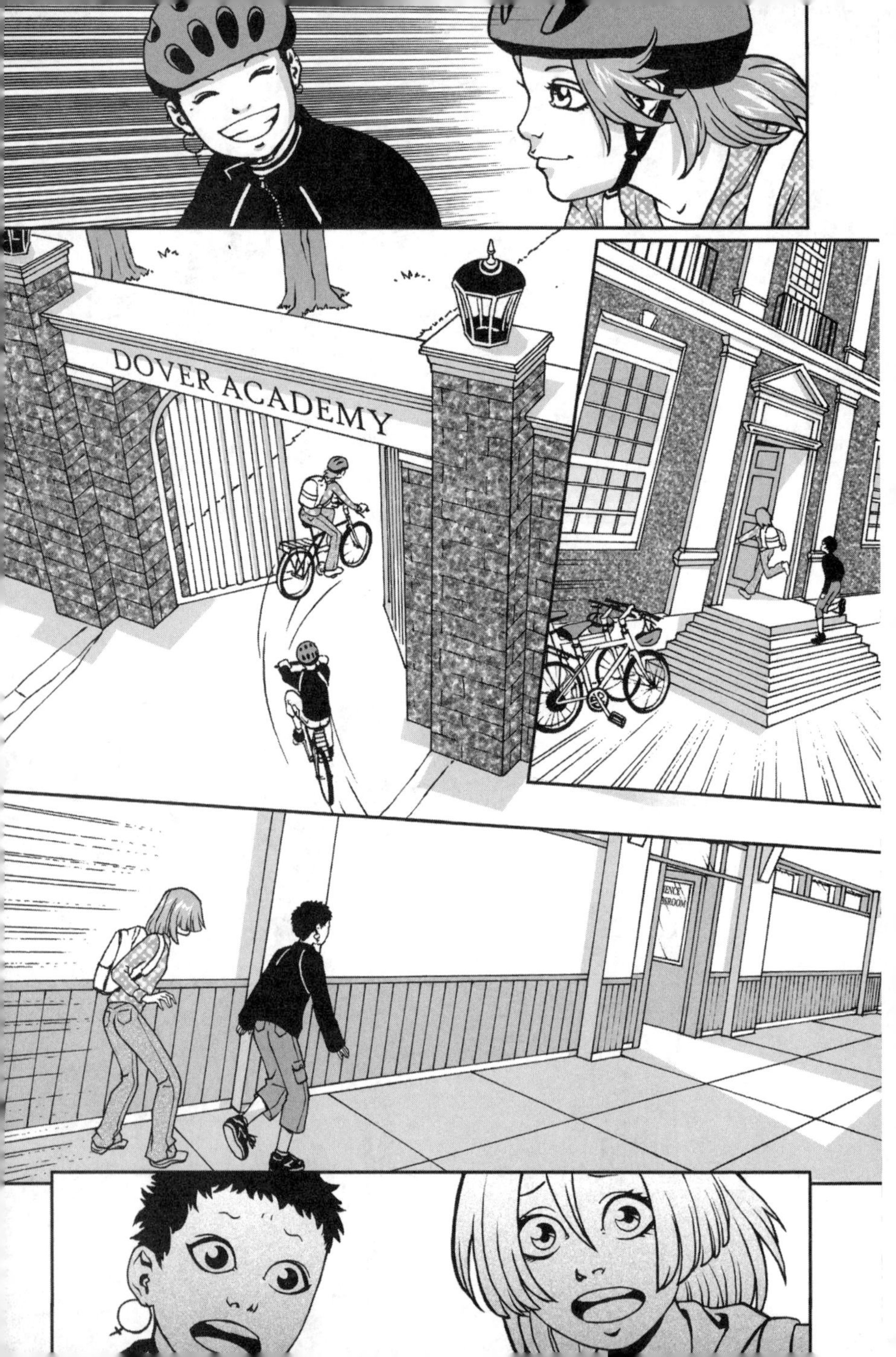
DOVER ACADEMY

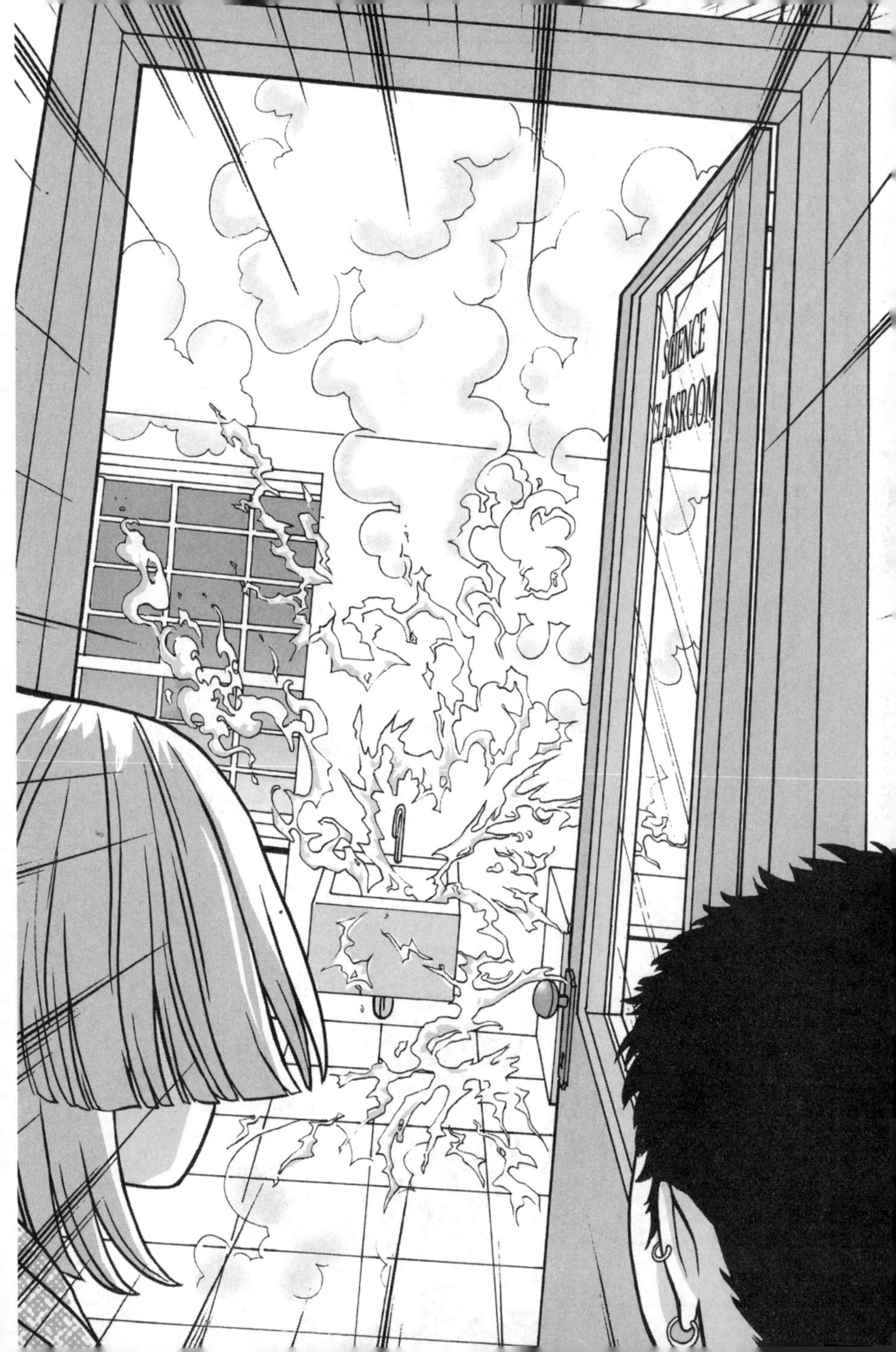
SCIENCE
CLASSROOM

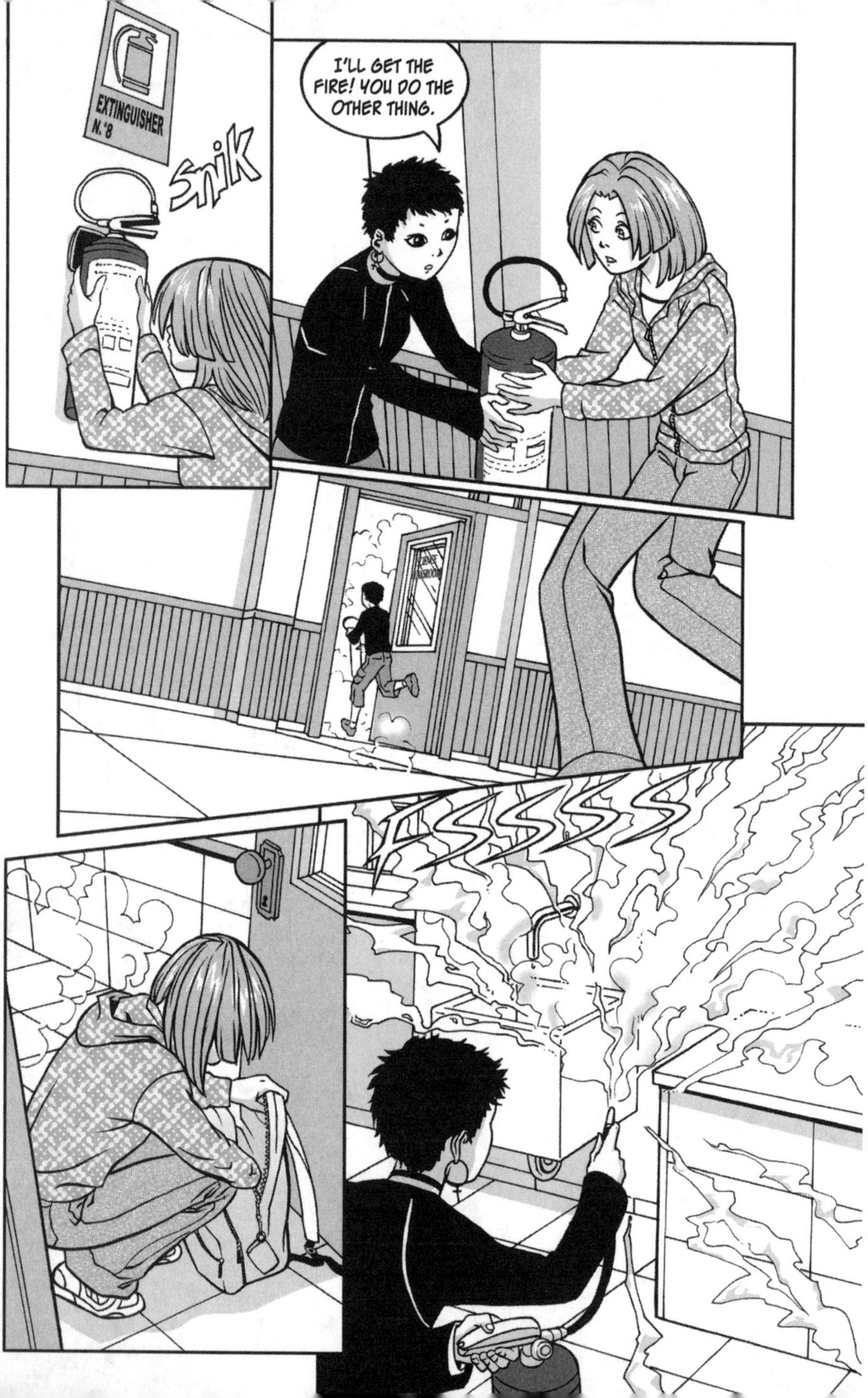
EXTINGUISHER
N.°8
SNIK
I'LL GET THE FIRE! YOU DO THE OTHER THING.
FSSSSS

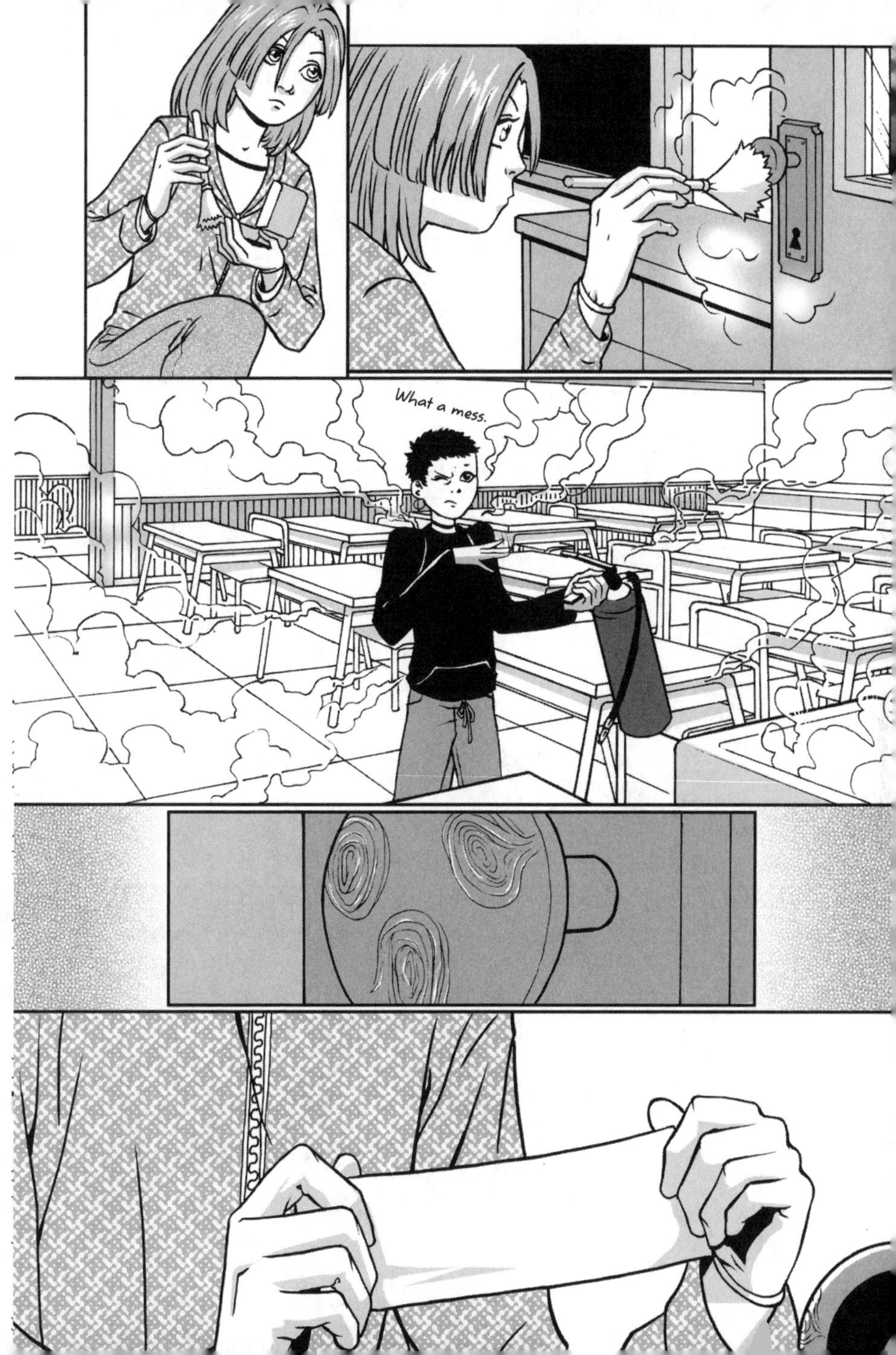
What a mess.

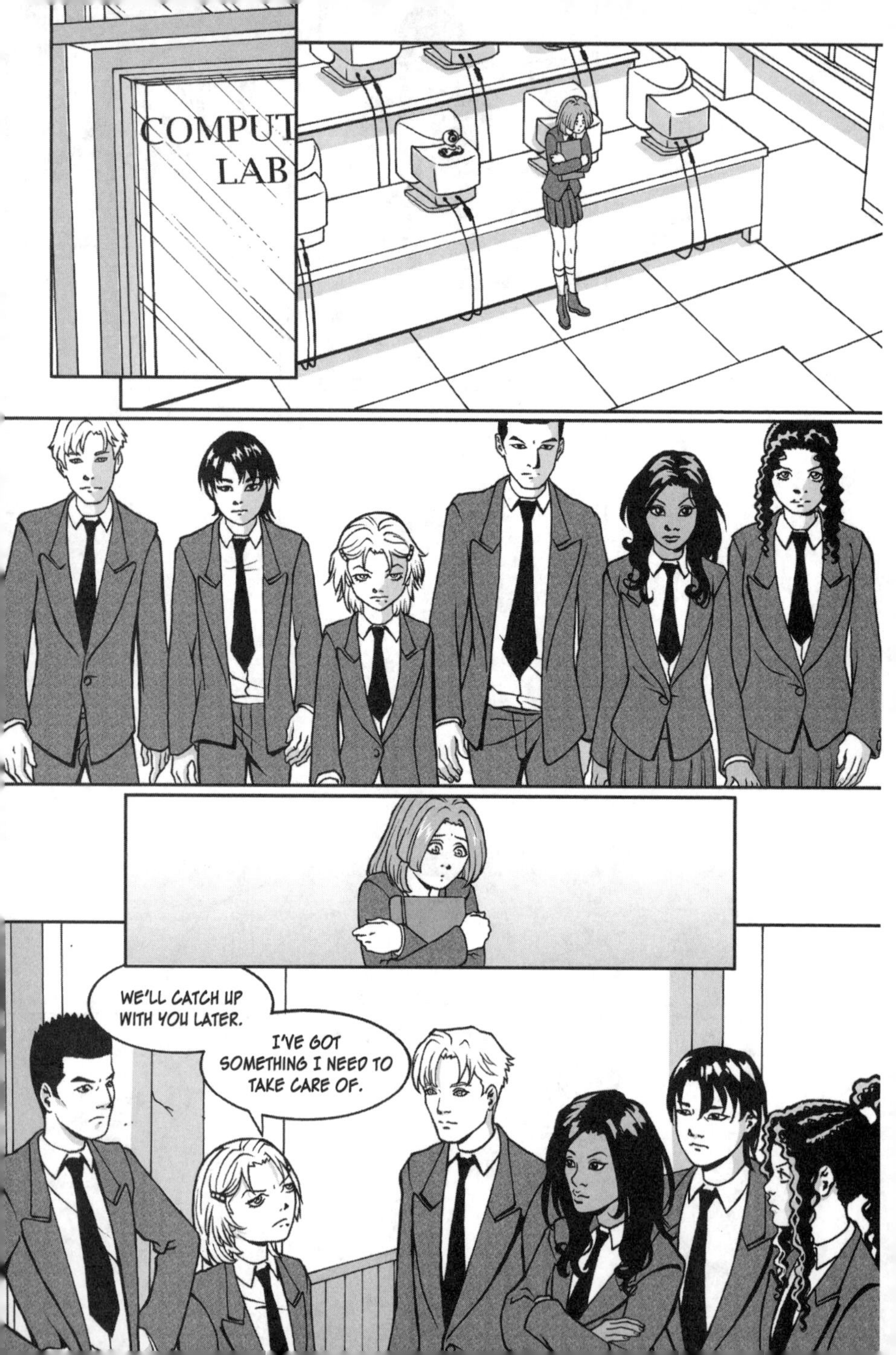
COMPUT
LAB
WE'LL CATCH UP WITH YOU LATER.
I'VE GOT SOMETHING I NEED TO TAKE CARE OF.

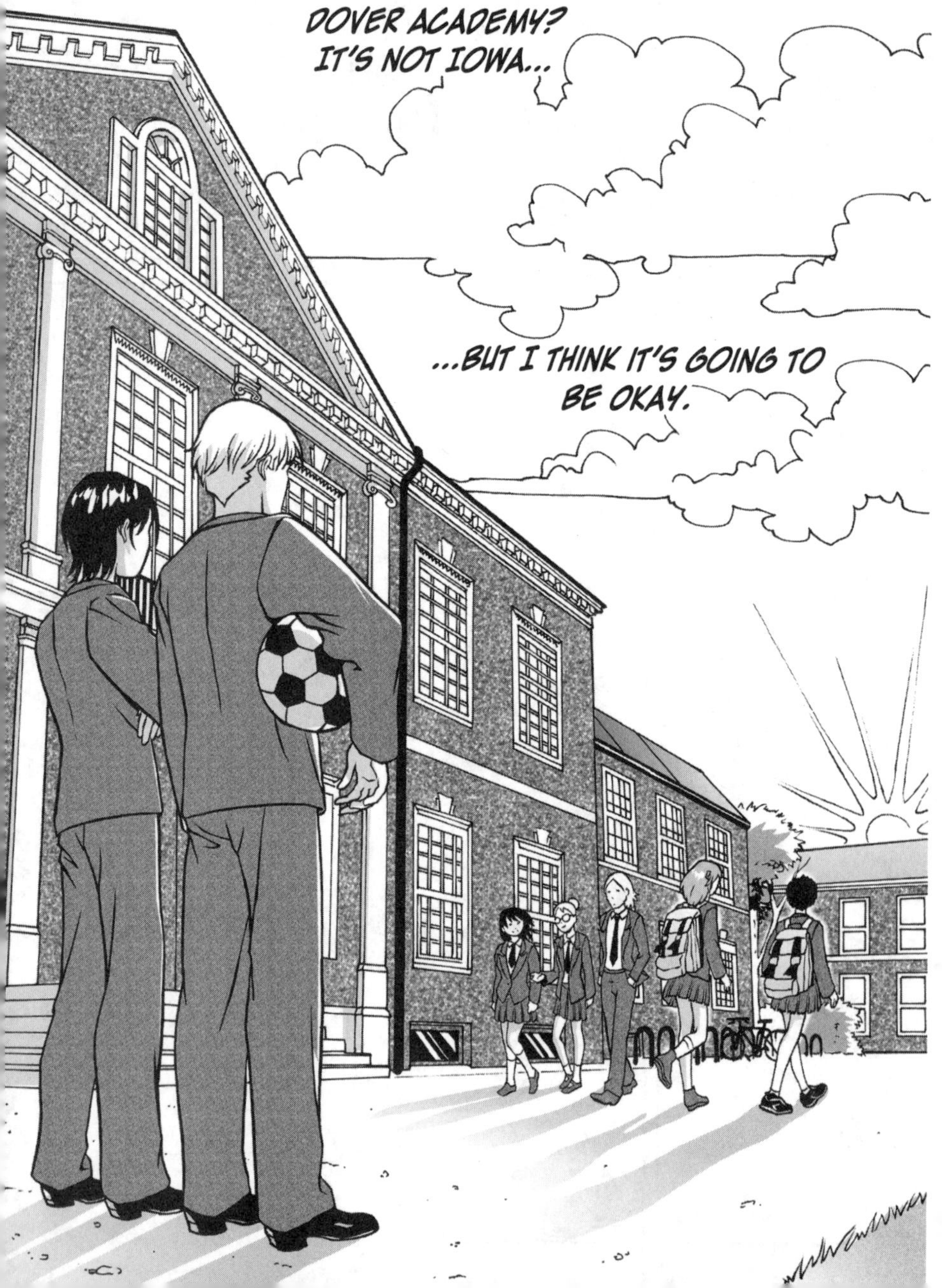
DOVER ACADEMY? IT'S NOT IOWA...
...BUT I THINK IT'S GOING TO BE OKAY.

# Kat & mouse

## ② tripped

*When Kat and Mouse's class takes a trip to an art museum, a painting is stolen. Is it just a classmate's prank getting out of hand, or are they stuck in the museum with a real, dangerous criminal? Kat and Mouse are in the big city and on the case!*

# Try This at Home!

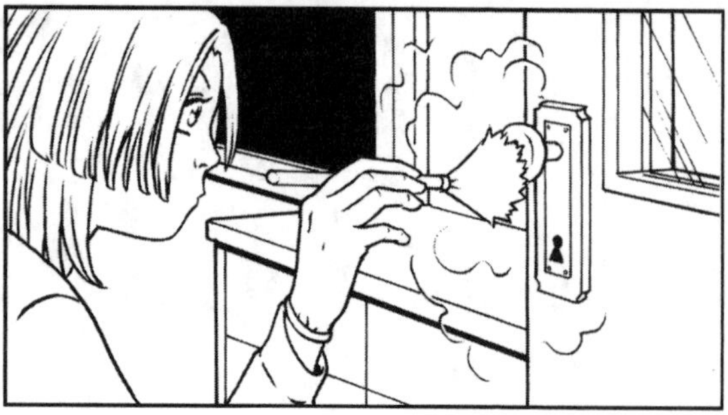

**Want to dust for fingerprints the way Kat & Mouse do in Chapters 3 and 4? Here's how!**

**You'll need:**

- A package of index cards
- A washable inkpad (make sure it's not dried out!)
- A clean, dry, fine paintbrush or makeup brush
- Clear adhesive tape
- Cocoa powder (unsweetened--the kind used for baking)
- Newspapers

First, get a record of your family's fingerprints. Have them lightly touch each of their fingers (both hands) on the inkpad, then press the fingers from each hand onto a separate index card--one card per hand, two per family member. Make sure you write names at the top of each card, so you won't forget who's who!

If you look hard at the fingerprints your family made, you'll notice that each falls under one of the seven types shown here. Can you match up each fingerprint with its type?

Sticky fingers make the best prints, so first try fingerprinting the drinking glasses your family uses during dinner (note: glass works a lot better than plastic for this).

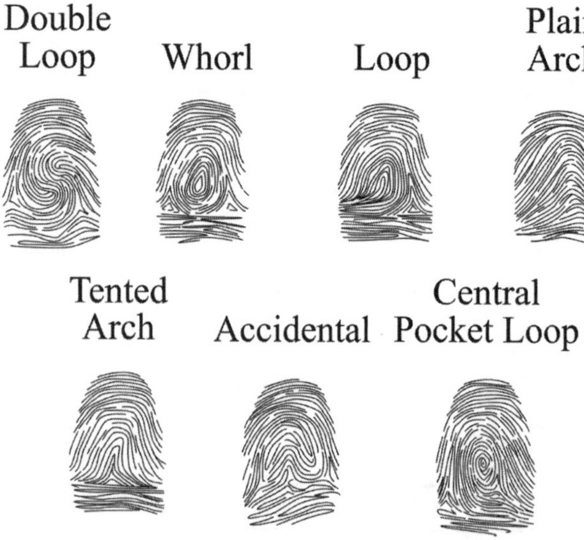

Double Loop
Whorl
Loop
Plain Arch
Tented Arch
Accidental
Central Pocket Loop

Shuffle the dirty glasses so you don't remember who was drinking out of which. Put newspapers under the place you'll do the dusting, then dip your dry brush into the cocoa powder and gently dust it over the area where hands would touch the glass. A light touch is important--if you brush too hard, you'll just smudge everything. Also, keep your face away from the dusting. Trust us, cocoa is not something you want in your eyes or up your nose.

The cocoa powder will stick to the residue left by the fingerprints, but not to the glass. To "lift" the print, cover it with the sticky side of the clear tape, then carefully peel the tape off and stick it down on a new index card--one card per glass.

Now, see if you can match the prints you lifted from the drinking glasses to the "index" prints your family did with the ink! Oh, and don't forget to wash the glasses and put everything away when you're done. Parents are much more forgiving about home experiments if they don't have to clean up after them.

This method works best on hard surfaces like drinking glasses, refrigerator doors, cabinets, and doorknobs. For darker surfaces, you can use talcum powder instead of cocoa. For softer surfaces, more advanced techniques are needed. Using chemicals, crime labs can get fingerprints off items like newspapers or leather jackets, and techniques like iodine fuming can be used for spy work, since it causes the prints to show up briefly, then disappear again.

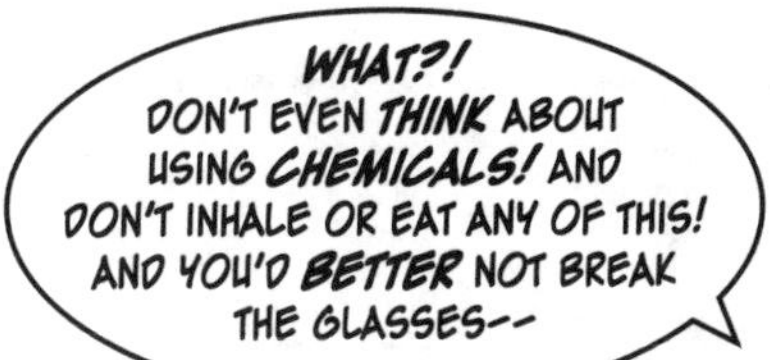

95

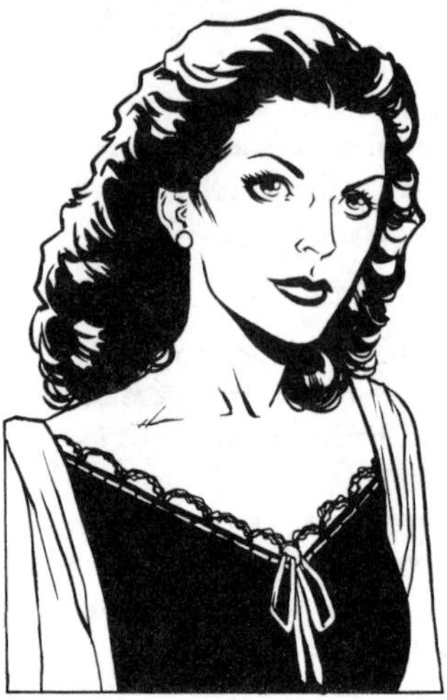

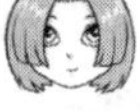

## KAT'S HEROES 1: HEDY LAMARR

The "Most Beautiful Woman in Films," Hedy Kiesler--stage name Hedy Lamarr--starred in 25 films from 1938-1954. She also made five films in Germany in the '30s, and was a heartbreaker even then--reportedly, a German nobleman committed suicide after she broke off their engagement.

Hedy then married wealthy arms dealer Fritz Mandl. Hedy had lots of ideas for improving the engineering of Fritz' weapons systems, but Fritz refused to listen to a "little woman." Hedy soon fled him and Nazi Germany in 1938, by sneaking out dressed up as her maid.

On a cruise ship to the U.S., she negotiated an acting contract with Louis B. Mayer, the most important producer in Hollywood. She stepped off onto American soil as MGM's next film star--but while audiences only saw a beautiful face, Hedy was far more passionate about her inventions.

She and co-inventor George Antheil created a radio system for guiding torpedoes, and she gave the patent to the American government to support the war effort. Although the system wasn't used much in the war due to technology limitations at the time, it has since become the basis for Spread Spectrum, on which almost all wireless phone and Internet communication depends.

Hedy also invented a small cube that could be put into drinks to carbonate them, so American soldiers could have sodas at the front lines!

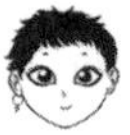

## MOUSE'S HEROES 1: EILEEN COLLINS

Some of NASA space shuttle commander Eileen Collins' fondest childhood memories were of driving out with her dad to watch the planes take off and land at the airport near her home in upstate New York. But she didn't decide to become a pilot until high school, when she read stories about pilots in the Vietnam War who were shot down and captured as POWs, then escaped.

Eileen knew it would be difficult to qualify as an Air Force test pilot, but she had always been a hard worker: Her parents had made her work for her allowance, and she had cleaned classrooms in order to afford tuition at Catholic school. So she saved any extra money she had for flying lessons. Her dream came true with her first flying lesson, taught by an instructor who had been a Phantom F-4 pilot in Vietnam... and who treated her as an equal.

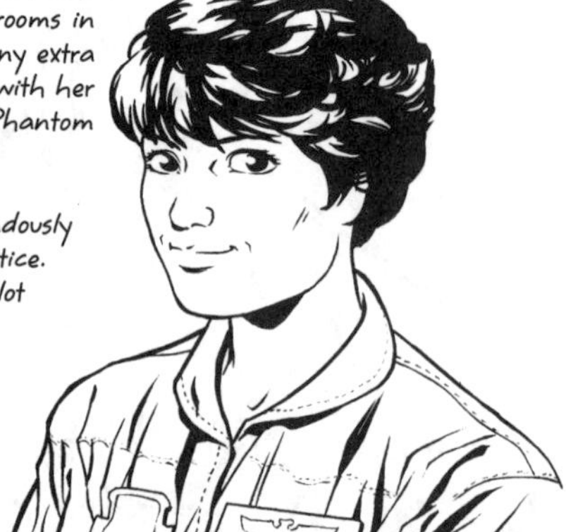

Eileen wasn't much for sports, but she was a tremendously talented pilot, flying solo after only eight hours of practice. After graduating from the Air Force Undergraduate Pilot Training Program at Vance Air Force Base in 1979, she was an instructor pilot and assistant mathematics professor--until 1990, when she passed NASA's extremely competitive selection program.

Eileen was the first woman pilot of the Space Shuttle, and has logged four space missions and over 872 hours in space.